LUCIFER'S FLOOD

LINDA RIOS BROOK

REALMS
A STRANG COMPANY

Most STRANG COMMUNICATIONS Book Group products are available at special quantity discounts for bulk purchase for sales promotions, premiums, fundraising, and educational needs. For details, write Strang Communications Book Group, 600 Rinehart Road, Lake Mary, Florida 32746, or telephone (407) 333-0600.

LUCIFER's FLOOD by Linda Rios Brook
Published by Realms
A Strang Company
600 Rinehart Road
Lake Mary, Florida 32746
www.strangbookgroup.com

Design Director: Bill Johnson
Cover design by studiogearbox.com
Cover Image: © Kamil Vojnar, Photographer, Getty Images

Library of Congress Cataloging-in-Publication Data:

Brook, Linda Rios.
  Lucifer's flood / Linda Rios Brook.
      p. cm.
  ISBN 978-1-59979-314-6
  1. Bible stories, English--O.T. Genesis. 2. Devil. 3.
Creation. 4. Bible. O.T. Genesis--History of Biblical
events. I. Title.
  BS550.3.B76 2008
  231.7'65--dc22

                                    2008007139

09 10 11 12 13 — 10 9 8 7 6 5 4
Printed in the United States of America

A NOTE TO THE READER

This book is fantasy. It is not intended to be regarded as a theological treatise. Having said that, allow me to share why I wrote it.

I believe, as do many lettered scholars and ministers, that there was a span of time of unknown length between Genesis 1:1 and Genesis 1:2. The possible mistranslation of a single word holds the potential to shift our paradigm in understanding the war in heaven, the creation of the earth, and the exile of Lucifer. "And the earth was without form, and void; and darkness was upon the face of the deep" (Gen. 1:2, KJV).

Many theologians argue that the word *was* should have been translated "had become." Known as the gap theory, this position assumes that a cataclysmic event may have occurred on the earth before the Spirit of God hovered over the chaotic deep and restored creation. *The Chumash: The Stone Edition* (Jewish commentary on the Torah) translates Genesis 1:1–2 in this way: "In the beginning of God's creating the heavens and the earth, the earth had become a confused, desolate, empty place, a wilderness."

If this translation is accurate, what happened to the earth to bring it to such devastation? Our understanding of the Genesis account may be likened to arriving late at the theater, only in time to see the start of the second act of the drama. We don't know what the first act was about, or even that there was a first act. Even if we presuppose a traditional interpretation of Genesis to be the full account of a finite creation in need of no further investigation, it still does not satisfactorily address what an infinite God might have been doing before creating the heavens and the earth.

While this story is fiction and should not be interpreted any other way, in weaving the tale, I—and the editors—have taken great care not to mishandle the biblical accounts contained herein. Jewish commentary (mentioned above) and *Dictionary of Jewish Lore and Legend* (Thames & Hudson LTD, London) have influenced the treatment of the men and women of Genesis. If their characterizations cause them to appear too "human," it is intentional. My desire is not to persuade believers to any other point of view, but to challenge the assumptions of those who do not believe but desperately wish they could.

This is a story about rebellion and consequences. It is about demonic strategy to disrupt and destroy the people of God. But ultimately, it is a story about the unrelenting love, grace, mercy, and determination of a sovereign God in pursuit of His errant children.

—Linda Rios Brook

CHAPTER 1

JERUSALEM WAS MYSTICAL at night. Samantha Yale stood at her office window. She never tired of the view of the golden dome reflecting the pure light of a full moon. Her days started early and ended late, but she never failed to take a minute at the end of it all to appreciate the majesty and beauty of the most intriguing city on the earth. Tonight was different though. She was waiting for someone.

She had learned to be cautious about strangers. The nature of her work tended to attract two kinds of people: the serious scholars, those interested in communication forms of prehistoric races; and the not-to-be-taken-seriously kind. These were the ones who would waste her time if she let them. On first contact with an unknown person it wasn't easy to tell which tribe he or she represented. She had learned to weed them out quickly. When the conversation turned to aliens, UFO abduction, or government conspiracy, she quickly ended the meeting, ushering them out the door with a promise to pass the information on to others.

"I need to get a life," she said as she watched for some sign of her expected visitor. The street below was empty. She assumed he would park in the visitor's space right in front of the building, but no beams from oncoming headlights announced an approaching car. A glance at her watch told her he was not late yet. She continued to watch and wait.

Stealthily as a cat, a man in a trench coat stepped through the ground fog and hesitated beneath the pale light of the street lamp. "Where did he come from?" she asked herself as she watched him look around as if checking to see if someone followed him. He seemed uncomfortable with the large satchel under his arm, shifting it from one side of his body to the other as if expecting it to be snatched from him by some thief hiding in the shadows. A dog barked in the distance; he jumped, almost dropping the satchel.

She watched him as he turned in circles, apparently unsure of which way to go. Hoping this wasn't whom she was waiting for, she was beginning to get a sense of the tribe he belonged to. "Please, God, don't let that be him."

Finally making up his mind which way to go, the man made for the steps leading into the building of the university and rang the entry bell for after-hours visitors.

"I knew it." She groaned. "It's him. He probably doesn't have a car. He's probably not an archaeologist either. I shouldn't have agreed to this."

Samantha moved toward the door, took a deep breath, and turned the knob as soon as she heard the first tap. The man looked like he had slept in his clothes. He was disheveled and seemed confused that she had opened the door before he completed knocking on it. Academics were often careless with their appearance. She had known more than a few who couldn't be bothered with pressed pants and combed hair. His persona was not really that different from many of the older rabbis and professors who roamed the hallways of the university. Still, something about him was unsettling.

"Mr. Eman, I assume." She opened the door a little wider.

"Yes, Dr. Yale." He paused and did a visual sweep of her office before stepping in. "Thank you for seeing me on such short notice." Samantha knew good manners meant offering to take his coat, but she did not want him to feel comfortable enough to prolong his visit.

"Please sit down." She motioned toward a wingback chair in front of her antique desk. He waited until she sat on the other side of the desk before sitting himself.

"What can I do for you, Mr. Eman?" She glanced at her watch again.

"Dr. Yale, I read in the *Jerusalem Post* about your work," he paused waiting for her response. She gave none. "About the Torah codes."

"Yes, I know, Mr. Eman. You mentioned that on the phone. How can I help you?"

He shifted his eyes from side to side then down to the bottom of her desk as if he had suddenly forgotten why he was there.

"How can I help you?" she repeated.

He jumped as if startled. "I'm sorry," he paused. "Languages of antiquity—that is your expertise, isn't it?"

She nodded.

"Then I have something to show you."

"You said that when we talked. Is it in your bag?" She looked at the satchel he held firmly in his lap.

"Yes," he said making no movement to open it.

"Mr. Eman, you said you had scrolls you wanted me to see. Are they in your bag?"

"Yes, I have them right here," he spoke in a low, secretive tone. "I want to know if you know what they are." He carefully unlocked the bag and removed a rolled parchment, laying it on her desk.

Her archaeology training restrained her from picking up what was obviously a very old document. "Where did you get it?" she asked, rummaging in her desk drawer for a magnifying glass.

"What do you mean?" he asked.

"I mean where did you get it?" She laid the glass down on her desk, folded her hands, and leaned forward. "No trick questions, Mr. Eman. I simply want to know where you got it. I cannot help you if you won't tell me where this came from."

"I found it—them. There's more than one." He pointed to the open satchel. "I have more of them right here."

"Where did you find them?" she tried again.

"In a cave near Hebron."

She thought about asking him what he was doing in such a cave but thought better of it. "Better not to draw this out just yet," she thought.

"Are you going to unroll it?" He seemed anxious.

"I'm afraid to do that." She held her magnifying glass over the scroll, looking for any evidence of a hoax. "I don't know how old it is or what it is. Opening it might cause damage."

"No, it's OK," he answered quickly. "I unrolled it once already."

Her suspicion was proving to be true. Obviously he had no specialized archaeological training. She sighed at the carelessness of nonspecialists who were forever destroying important evidence with their careless treatment of ancient objects.

"You might have destroyed it."

"I didn't. You'll see. Open it." He pushed the scroll a little closer to her.

Her suspicions grew as the idea of a hoax seemed more and more likely. "Why did you bring this to me, Mr. Eman?"

"Because of your work with the Torah codes."

"I see." She was becoming more convinced he was one of the UFO tribe.

He became nervous when she said nothing more. Pushing the scroll slightly toward her again, his tone seemed almost urgent. "Please open it, Dr. Yale. This is older than the Torah."

"What?" she had not expected such a comment. "Very unlikely, sir, but even if it were, how could you possibly know?"

Unsure of her motivation, her natural curiosity as a scientist or his escalating anxiety, she carefully untied the leather string that held the scroll and gently rolled it open. Feeling no fragility of a document that might crumble beneath her fingers, she unrolled it a little more.

"What kind of material is this?" she asked, never looking up from the scroll.

"Parchment, I suppose," he answered.

"No, it's not."

"No? Are you sure, Dr. Yale?"

"I'm sure it's not parchment." Gently she rubbed the material between her fingers. "If it were parchment it would have cracked and turned to dust with the careless handling you've displayed here. That alone argues against it being as old as the Torah. I'm afraid it isn't a genuine relic, Mr. Eman. Sorry."

"No, I mean, yes, it is," He shifted to the edge of his chair, causing her to sit back slightly in hers. "Look at it. It has writing on it."

Reluctantly, she picked up her glass and examined the inscription. She leaned closer to the scroll, seeing for the first time the faded but clearly visible markings that suggested writing. It was not the work of an amateur forger. After several minutes, he broke her concentration.

"It is writing, isn't it?" he pressed.

"It's more than an alphabet," she responded leaning back in her chair and pressing her fingers together. "It's cuneiform, Mr. Eman. Do you know what that is?"

He shook his head.

"Cuneiform comes from two Latin words: *cunaus*, meaning wedge; and *forma*, meaning shape. Individual words, like this one..." Without touching the document, she pointed with the tip of her pen at a rectangular shape, "...are called pictographs because the word looks like what it means." Moving the pen across the scroll, she continued. "These wedges and hooks are called ideographs, which also represent words. This line of characters is an ideogram, which represents a concept." She paused to see if he understood her explanation. Assuming from his silence that he didn't, she tried an analogy.

"Think of it like this: Consider this desk we're sitting at. If I said to you, 'This desk cost me an arm and a leg,' what do you think I mean?"

"The desk cost a lot of money."

"Exactly. You would not have thought I had cut off my arm and leg in exchange for it. That's how an ideogram works. It takes words that mean one thing and strings them together until they present a different concept altogether. To translate cuneiform into a modern language means mastering a large syllabic alphabet as well as a large number of ideograms, which also means very few people alive today can do it."

"But you can," Eman looked intently into her eyes.

Tapping her fingers together as if measuring out her words, she said, "Yes, Mr. Eman. I suppose I could. There's only one problem. Parchment was unknown when cuneiform was used. It was etched into clay tablets. How do you suppose it came to be written on this strange material?"

"Will you do it?" he asked, ignoring her question.

She stood and walked to a nearby table and poured a glass of water. He waved his hand to decline the one she offered him.

"I won't do it until you tell me more about where you got them."

"I can't." His voice was distraught. Standing up to face her, he continued. "Look at me, Dr. Yale. I promise you I didn't steal them. And I know you've figured out that I'm not capable of creating this caliber of forgery."

"Why are you so desperate to have them translated?"

Eman slumped back down in his chair. Putting his head in his hands, he shook it from side to side. "Because it's a diary."

She suppressed a smile. "A diary? Whose diary?"

"Please, Dr. Yale. I can't tell you anything more. Just translate the first scroll. Just one, then you'll see."

Her training and experience shouted, "Fakery!" into her brain. Whoever he was and whatever he had were bound to be part of a con game she had not yet figured out. "I should have thrown him out," she thought as she watched him with his head resting in his hands. But there was something pathetic about him. He didn't seem capable of a complicated plot.

"One scroll," she agreed, overriding training and experience with a gut-level intuition that told her to pay attention to what was before her.

"Thank you, thank you, Dr. Yale." He jumped to his feet and reached for her hand and shook it fervently. "You'll see. When can you do it?"

"I'm not sure. I'll get to it as soon as I can. Give me your card and I'll call you."

His face fell. "I don't have a card or a phone. I'll have to call you." Leaving the scroll on the desk and fastening his satchel, he hurried to leave.

"No phone? Not even a cell phone?"

"No, no." He stumbled as he caught the satchel strap on the arm of the chair almost turning it over. "I'll call you. In twenty-four hours I'll call you." He moved to the door.

"Impossible," she began, but before she could protest or ask any more questions, he was gone.

Samantha was still standing when at last she shook her head as if reviving from a trance. "What happened here?" She surveyed the empty room, confused as to how this strange man could have disappeared so quickly. She carefully opened the heavy oak door and peered out to see if he might be lurking in the hallway. Satisfied the corridor was empty, she closed and locked the door and returned to her desk. Staring at the scroll and trying to decide what to do, she became aware of the strange disquiet she felt toward it.

Through her open window she could hear the chiming of a faraway clock. "I shouldn't do anything with this until tomorrow." Half rising from her seat, she abruptly sat back down as if an invisible hand had rested on her shoulder, compelling her to stay where she was. Fingering the scroll, but reluctant to open it, she attempted to reconcile her uneasiness with the excited curiosity of an explorer rising up within her.

"You don't need this distraction, Samantha Yale," she said aloud, as if hearing her own voice would convince her that whatever it was, tomorrow was soon enough to find out. "Thou shalt not kid thyself, Sam. You know you wouldn't sleep anyway."

It had always been like that for her—captivated from her youth by the intrigue of the past. "What is, *was*," her mentor had insisted. "What was, *is*." She closed her eyes to remember the wisdom in his eyes as he taught her. "You cannot understand the end, Samantha, until you understand the beginning."

But where was the beginning? How far back could the human mind go in search of it? Gently unfurling the ancient document, she took it captive, placing paperweights at each corner to forbid its escape until it gave up its secrets. With the magnifying glass in hand, she looked intently at each marking as words emerged and came alive with the voice of someone long ago who beckoned her to listen.

CHAPTER 2

LL RIGHT," she said as she gave in to the lure of antiquity. "Talk to me." Taking her pen in hand, she began a careful translation.

It's not like I didn't try to fight. I swung the sword with all my might, but Rafael did not even duck. He ripped the blade from my grasp and wielded it right back at me as if it were nothing and I was less. If utter terror had not propelled me to jump much higher than I was able under normal circumstances, well, that would have been the end of me right there. Some of us were warriors, and some of us were not. I was among the "nots." No sane person would confuse me with a warrior. That's why Rafael lost interest in me so quickly and went after a more worthy opponent. He realized I was neither a threat nor a trophy.

I may not have a lot of courage, but I do have common sense. I quickly began looking for someplace to hide. The safest place for me would be the throne room—if I could make it there. Not a chance. From a distance I could see it was so heavily guarded that it would be certain destruction to try to break through that line.

I was afraid to stand up and run lest I get in the way of those flashing swords. Abandoning any pretension of pride I might have once had, I dropped on my belly and crawled like a worm until I found an unguarded rock where I curled in a ball and tried to make myself as small as possible. The lightning flashes from the swords were so terrifying that I got a cramp trying to force myself lower still behind the rock that couldn't possibly protect me anyway. With my eyes shut tight, I waited for it to be over.

That's why I didn't see what happened. I was too afraid to look until the thunderous crashing around me became so horrible that what I couldn't see scared me more than what I could. Sensing a pause in the action, and hoping I wouldn't make my situation worse, I opened one eye to see if I could get away before the fighting started up again.

When I looked up and saw Michael the archangel and captain of the host not three feet from where I was hiding, I squealed as if I had been sliced in half. Michael's eyes flamed, and his bulging muscles pulsed as he swung his sword in my direction. I fell over and pretended to be dead.

With my eyes closed again, I didn't move a feather as I listened to the sounds of war around me. Michael never missed, so I knew I was not his target, but it didn't take long to figure out who was. It was Damon, the platoon leader, who had met the might of Michael's sword. I swallowed the scream rising up in my throat and continued to play dead.

I was desperate to find out how badly Damon might have been hurt. If it wasn't too bad, maybe he would give me cover while I ran away. I cracked my eye again in time to see Damon's severed head roll across the ground and land right on top of my left foot. Playing dead was no longer working for me.

I nudged Damon's head away with my toe, then jumped up and ran, flew, stumbled, and tumbled back toward the throne room, babbling all the way. I knew I must get through somehow. What would I say? I would plead for mercy. I would plead insanity. I would grovel at the feet of the guarding angels. Call me a traitor or call me a coward, I did not care. I was working out my plea in my head as I ran along the streets of gold, dodging the lightning bolts bursting forth from both sides.

I was almost there, but I was too late. A thundering silence settled in like a fog over the city of God. As quickly as it had begun, the war in heaven was suddenly over.

CHAPTER 3

S AMANTHA LOOKED IN the mirror over the lavatory of her private bath—one of the few perks she had as a fellow at the university. With her tousled black hair and faded makeup from the day before, she knew she was fast beginning to resemble the absent-minded rabbis and professors who slept in their clothes. She remembered how her mother had told her as a teenager that African American girls like her had naturally beautiful skin and didn't need costly cosmetics like her friends painted on their faces. "Mama, you were so wrong," she thought as she tried to freshen her tired face with a splash of water.

She had not left her office in more than twenty-four hours. A lone cookie from a box lunch days before was all she had eaten since beginning the translation. Now she waited eagerly for Wonk Eman's phone call.

Pacing the length of her office and occasionally looking out the window for some sign of him, her mind raced through the possible implications if the scrolls were authentic. At last the phone rang. She picked it up and waited before speaking.

"Is it you, Dr. Yale?" asked the whispering voice on the other end.

"Yes, Mr. Eman, it's me."

"Please call me 'Wonk.' I am so uncomfortable with Mr. Eman."

"As you wish." She did not suggest he call her "Samantha."

"Did you read it?" he asked anxiously.

"Yes, I did. When can I get the other scrolls?"

Silence.

"Are you still there, Mr....uh...Wonk?" she wondered if the connection had been lost.

"I'm still here." He paused again. "I'm sorry, Dr. Yale. I hadn't thought this far ahead. I wasn't sure you would translate the scroll. Now that you have, I'm not sure what to do next."

"The first thing you must do is bring me the other scrolls." She hoped she did not seem overbearing; he was such a nervous type, and she did not want to scare him away.

Silence.

Intentionally using her softest tone, she prodded him. "Wonk, I cannot translate the scrolls if I don't have them. You do want them translated, don't you?"

"Yes, of course," he replied. "They must be translated."

"Can you bring them to me—today?" she gently pressed.

"I will have them delivered to you. I can't come myself. Someone could be watching me. There could be consequences."

"Now, listen, Wonk," she struggled to keep her tone soft. "You assured me the scrolls had not been stolen. If they're contraband, I can't touch them."

"No, no, nothing like that. They belong to me."

"Then bring them to me yourself. You should be careful about sending them by messenger. If you must, then use a delivery service like FedEx—or an agency that issues a tracking number so they can't disappear."

"I will do it. By tomorrow I will have them to you. But you must be in your office to receive them. They can't be left to anyone else."

"Don't worry, Wonk. I will stay in my office tomorrow until they are delivered."

"Yes." His voice seemed unconnected to his thoughts. "Yes, of course, they must be translated. I know it must be done."

Samantha attempted to reassure him. "It is the right thing to do. I need to see all of them to ascertain the true historical value of such a discovery." She paused; hearing no response, she continued to affirm his decision. "After all, I know you are anxious to know what they will reveal."

"I already know, Dr. Yale."

CHAPTER 4

S AMANTHA ARRIVED AT her office much earlier than usual. Although the package would not be delivered until 10:00 a.m., she took no chances on missing an early delivery. No matter how many times she looked at her watch, the minutes passed at the same speed. Finally, she heard a knock on her door.

"Dr. Samantha Yale?" asked the delivery man in a blue uniform. She nodded.

"Sign here." Giving her a copy of the delivery confirmation, he carried the box into her office and set it down on the small conference table. "This OK?"

"Yes, right there is fine. Thank you very much." She quickly ushered him out the door.

Taking a letter opener and a pair of scissors from her desk drawer, she began the task of cutting through the tape that bound the box on all sides. Lifting the lid and removing the bubble wrap, she paused a moment to consider how she should remove the scrolls. She hoped they were in some kind of order.

The scrolls had been carefully arranged in layers of four across. Assuming this to be the chronological order, she took them out one by one and laid them cautiously across the rectangular table. "How will I keep them in order if I have to move them?" Looking around her office for a solution, she spied a pad of Post-it notes on her desk.

"Why not?" She took the pages from the pad, numbered them, and attached one to each scroll. "Twenty-first-century bookmarks meet antiquity."

She carried the first scroll to her desk and carefully rolled it out. She paused for a moment to consider the task she was about to undertake. Looking intently at the markings on the strange parchment, she thought, "If this is a hoax, it is artfully done."

Taking her pen in hand, she began to unravel the secrets of—she wasn't exactly sure of what. An angel? A deranged person of long ago? Her anticipation escalated as she set about the search for the elusive writer.

I have a name. But no one has called me by name for a long, long time, so I don't suppose it matters much what it is. No one could understand what happened to me on that awful day. It was not my fault, but I was blamed and punished as if I were as guilty as the rest. Let me remain hidden in the shadow of anonymity. At first, I dared to hope there might be some restitution if I just had the chance to explain how such a disaster came about—as if confessing would somehow bring redemption for the foolish and tragic thing I did that, let me be clear, was not my fault. If any modicum of redemption were available to me, I would risk anything to attain it. But it is not so. Redemption is not possible for me. It was not only a terrible mistake, but also an eternal one.

None of what happened is fair to me. Why should redemption be available to humans and no one else? What makes humans more worthy than I am? I have feelings. I tried my best. I made one mistake—just one—ever. Shouldn't I be entitled to a second chance? When I tell you what happened, you will see it was not my fault.

You can only understand the lunacy of the rebellion if you first know about Him. Everything begins and ends with Him, so I shall try to tell you what He is like. He is called the Ancient of Days, Elohim, Yahweh, Jehovah, I Am, and God. He is without beginning and without end. He did not come to be; He was, He is, and He will always be. His existence defies the limitations of the finite minds that He has created. His creation would call His name by what they saw Him do. And we, those who are like me, saw Him do marvelous things. Indeed, we were some of the earliest part of His creation. I don't know when we came to be or how we came to be, but suddenly we *were*, and it was as if we had always been. And so we knew Him as the Creator God who existed in three persons: Yahweh (the Father), Adonai (His Son), and Ruah Ha Kadosh (whoever He was because no one was ever sure). Three distinct beings and yet in such perfect oneness with one another that it never occurred to any of us that an outsider might be perplexed as to how such a thing could be. This is how it was; how it always was. Not one of us questioned how or why. They were One, and we were the host of heaven.

Adonai, His Son, was forever making things. I often wondered where He got His ideas. (Some thought He really didn't have any ideas of His own. They were His Father's wishes, and He just carried them out.) Whatever the case, one could never be sure what He was going to make next. For example, He would make a useful thing one day and the next make something that seemed to have no purpose at all. Like the planets—what was He thinking? After taking a look at a few of them, it was obvious to me He had truly not thought through what He planned to do with them before He started. As far as I could see, all but one were duds. Still, He kept on making them until a good part of the universe was cluttered with them. To me it seemed He just could not get the formula right.

The stars, on the other hand, were a good idea. We could see that right away. If nothing else, it gave Him a place to put the useless planets. Earth was the only one you would take out of the closet to show company.

I remember the awe in all of us the first time we really looked at Earth. It was beautiful. The blue and green oceans were teeming with life we had never imagined. The seas alone could have been a universe unto themselves. There in the depths of the waters were caverns so massive that they could have swallowed up any canyon on the surface of Earth. The mountain ranges deep beneath the surface dwarfed the magnificent ranges that spiraled above the land itself.

And let me tell you about the fish. Keep in mind that none of us had seen one before. To be sure, Adonai made many other life forms far more complex and interesting to look at. None of us truly appreciated the complicated engineering required to make a working model from fins, scales, and gills. He made it look simple, so naturally, we thought it was.

As far as I was concerned, this displayed an aspect of Adonai's character that defied understanding. He made thousands of them. Big, little, beautiful, funny looking, ferocious looking—every kind of fish you might imagine was there in the pristine waters of Earth. But that wasn't what fascinated me as much as the tiny ones that lived near the ocean's floor.

I couldn't believe the detail that went into making these little bitty creatures. No bigger than two or three inches at most, they lived in the coldest depths of the water, where humans would never go. Miniature works of art, painted with iridescent colors of chartreuse, aqua, green, blue, and yellow, and many of them with funny little headdresses that looked like hats made of fine feathers. Now here's why I marveled at these particular fish: Who was going to see them? Who would know they were there?

Nothing that lived above the waters could have descended to those depths. Not for eons could that happen, and then only in specialized craft much like what would eventually penetrate outer space. What was the point of putting so much creativity and beauty into something that no one would ever see?

Then I figured it out. He created them for Himself. He delighted in them whether any other living thing knew about the fish or not. He made them for His own pleasure.

Adonai liked the idea of fish so much that He did something I have rarely seen either He or His Father do. For the sake of the fish, He would defy one of the natural laws He had set in place to govern this new world. As nearly as I could tell, He did it solely to protect His fish.

Simply stated, here is how this law works: objects denser than water will sink in water. Ice is denser than water and should sink, but it does not. It floats.

Why? He must have been thinking about the parts of Earth where the waters would be so cold they turned to ice. Instead of sinking to the bottom, as, say, a rock would have, the ice stays on the top of the water. He wanted to protect His fish. The ice floats on top, and the fish continue to swim about in the waters below completely unaware of the amazing thing that has happened on their behalf.

Everyone in heaven came to the show when the comets were about. They looked like balls of fire shooting through the blackness of space at enormous speeds, dragging a tail of ice behind. It was breathtaking to watch. To be candid, the first time I saw a comet, I thought Adonai must have created it as a toy. I tell you there was no limit to His flair. For example, who would have thought of making a blue sky to match the seas? Skies were black, at least the ones we had seen before.

Then one day, He got an idea for something entirely different—and totally disruptive, I might add. How can I describe it? A rift? An interruption? Out of eternity where everything had been "now," He separated "now" into "past" and "present" and "future" and named it "time." Time had a beginning and passages and an end. Then He stepped out on the edge of time with His Father, and They observed what He had made. They liked the concept so much, They made everything else They created obedient to time. Even the universes and the stars and planets became governed by time. But the Godhead—the three of Them—were neither in time nor subject to time. And neither were we.

Time was to move forward, never backward, and at a steady pace with no sudden surges. It was then when He decided to put life on Earth. It was not going to be like anything They had done before. I don't know that we ever saw the three of Them as excited about any project as They were about this one.

We angels were not that interested in a new life form—especially if it were on one of the planets, even if it was the pretty one. That is until we found out the new life form would definitely be inferior to us and that He intended to set us as guardians over it.

Considering how things turned out, if He could do it over again, I'm pretty sure He would have made a different decision. It's His own fault that He couldn't have a do-over. If He hadn't made that law about the passing of time and that everything in time must pass with it, He could have reversed things and no one would have known the difference. But I digress.

Up until that day, we in the angelic realm never considered the notion that we could rule over anything. But once we did think about it, it made perfect sense. After all, we had beauty, strength, gifting, personality, intelligence, and free will. Why shouldn't we rule something—in the proper order, of course? The three made the decisions about the affairs of Earth, and we would carry them out. At first, we never thought to do it any other way.

And why would we? Our place in the universe was exalted, inferior to no other created thing, and our purpose was to do His bidding. In all of creation we were created the closest to the hearts of Yahweh and Adonai. The third member of their being, Ruah Ha Kadosh, did not actually interact with us. In fact, most times we were not really sure when He was around. He was not visible in the same ways the Father and the Son were visible. I suppose that sounds strange, but I don't mind telling you He *was* strange—mysterious even. At least it appeared so to us. It was easier to see the evidence that He had indeed been *somewhere* than to identify precisely where that *somewhere* might be. In other words, we could better point out where He *was* than explain where He *is*. But when anything important happened, He was always there.

Knowing humanity as I do, I'm certain that it's impossible for you to imagine what life was like for us before that tragic day. One of the design errors in human makeup is that history is completely wasted on you. You humans amaze us with your unquestioned belief that nothing grander than yourselves ever existed or that anything important ever happened before you came along. You really have no idea how it was.

It was much more majestic than you have imagined eternity and paradise to be. In fact, humans have such an impoverished view of what heaven is like that it amazes me that so many of you hope to go there when you die. If paradise were no more than you seem to think it is— cloud sitting, strumming harps, and singing hymns—I can't imagine why anyone would hope to spend eternity there. Why does that idea hold so much appeal for you, then, when nothing of the sort appeals to you now? It must be that you desire paradise only as an alternative to hell, but you are not really eager for it. Oh, but if you knew what it was really like, well, you would long for it as I most painfully do now. Neither your language nor mine is sufficient to describe heaven, so I shall not try. It is unspeakable. It is marvelous. I desperately long for the way it was when I was there with Them. But it is quite lost to me.

I wish I could explain what transpired in our hearts that dreadful day. I don't know how or why we began to change, but I do know when. From the first day we were set as celestial guardians over Earth, we were never the same. Lucifer pointed out to us that we had never before been allowed to realize our full potential, but now we were finally finding our true place. We liked being in *charge* of something. Not me, of course. No, thank you. I didn't want the responsibility of ruling over anything, but for some of the others, it was a different thrill altogether. I won't name names, of course, but let me tell you, some of them were absolutely giddy with the taste of power. It was embarrassing. That's when they began to believe a terrible thing. I will admit that hearing them talk about the possibilities did give one a bit of a tingle—even me. Lucifer helped us imagine ourselves in lofty ways completely contrary to our nature.

"Perhaps we were made to rule," he proposed.

"Lucifer's right," someone quipped. "Why should there be only one ruler?"

"Why shouldn't we rule ourselves? What in creation is more magnificent than us?"

The more they talked, the more they began to desire more than heaven. I began to wonder if we had somehow missed out on something. It wasn't long until we developed such pride in our own extraordinary selves that we started to consider how we could leave our sphere and its confinement. Lucifer was right.

"Why should there be limits for us? And who should decide what they are?" he asked.

Angels cannot handle ambition. Until Lucifer introduced us to the concept, our entire purpose for being was to carry out the plans of God; we never thought about doing anything else. Of all God had made, we were the most like Him. The heart of God was love, and He lavishly loved us. Perhaps that's why we were so foolish as to think our actions had no consequences. We had never disobeyed before. It had never been in anyone's imagination to do such a thing.

And that's how things would have remained if it hadn't been for Lucifer. It was entirely his fault. As one of the highest-ranking archangels, he had access to the throne room—something that none of the rest of us had. That's why we attached so much weight to what he said. Lucifer caused us to think about how exciting things might be if he were in charge. I don't know why, but I have to tell you there was a strange exhilaration about the idea. I found myself being swept along with the others in the excitement. Did we never once think there might be consequences for disobedience? Oh, yes, we did. But not really.

We were convinced that God's love for us was so great that it would not allow Him to bring punishment against us. Nonetheless, I was nervous.

"What if God isn't amused by Lucifer's political ideas? What if He thinks self-rule for us is rebellion?" I asked. "Will He just overlook it like nothing happened?"

"He can do nothing else. He is all about love, and He cannot deny His own nature," Lucifer assured us.

"Then are we safe to insist on our own way?" asked another. Lucifer nodded confidently, so we agreed that it must be true.

It was our knowledge of the depth of God's love for us that makes our betrayal all the more despicable. Oh, I know you think that you know about Lucifer. There was a time when we thought we did too. Believe me, you know nothing. You do not know his cunning or his hatred for all that lives on Earth. You do not know the extent of his willingness to corrupt, destroy, and steal. Perhaps that is the true reason I have decided to tell you what I saw happen. Lucifer is the source of my misery. If I seem bitter at times as I recount the events that forever changed heaven and Earth, well, it is because I most certainly am. It began with the rebellion of Lucifer.

Yahweh Himself would say Lucifer was the seal of perfection. He was wise, perfect, and beautiful. He glittered like a star when he moved about. He was clearly God's favorite. This is why none of us could have imagined what was about to happen. Even when the summons came, we were not alarmed. We were called to assembly in the high court of heaven, but that had happened before. God often called us to assembly when He had something new to share. He wasn't looking for our input, of course. I think He liked the looks on our faces when He amazed us with His inexhaustible creativity.

"What's the meeting about?" someone asked, but no one seemed to know.

We mused out loud as to what might be in store until the Ancient of Days took His place on the judgment seat of heaven. The atmosphere changed instantly. The angel next to me whispered, "Something is wrong."

"Wrong?" I whispered back. "How can anything be wrong in heaven?"

No one dared say anything more. Without being told to do so, we fell to our knees and folded our wings at the weight of His presence.

But something really was wrong. We had not seen Him like this before. The only word I can use to describe Him is *somber*. But how could that be? He was never somber. What was there to be somber about in heaven? We looked to Adonai for a clue, but His eyes betrayed nothing of what His Father was about to say.

Following God's gaze, I realized that Lucifer was standing alone among the kneeling angels. I nudged the angel next to me. "Tell him to bow down."

"He doesn't have to," he answered back.

"Do you see God's eyes?" I asked as quietly as possible.

The angel raised his head and saw the eyes of God sweeping across the legions bowed down before Him. Ducking back down, he quickly tapped the wing of the angel next to him, starting a moving line of nudges and whispers for Lucifer to bow down, but he would not.

"He isn't going to do it," the angel answered.

"Make him," I blurted out.

"Make him?" he asked incredulously, as if I had suggested some ridiculous thing, which, I suppose I had. Certainly none of us could make an archangel do anything.

"Then tell him to go stand by himself." I eked out the words and lowered my head as the cherubim who went before God ceased moving and lay flat on their faces as Omnipotence rose from His seat. Peering directly into Lucifer's eyes, as if no one else were in the room, God the Father opened His mouth to speak. The tone in His voice was heavy beyond bearing as He said to the archangel, "From the day of your creation, you were sheer perfection. Now look at what you have become. Evil has been found in you."

The pillars of the courtroom trembled at His words, and smoke rose above as the atmosphere became unstable. No one dared stand.

"What did God say?" The muttering swept through the kneeling angels.

"Evil? In Lucifer?" The accusation telegraphed through the whispers of the gathered host.

"Wait a minute," I interrupted. "What does God mean by *evil*? We don't know anything about *evil*."

For a moment the telegraphing stopped as the others realized what I said was true. Although it was clear from God's words that something was definitely wrong, no one in heaven could possibly have understood something that until now had not existed. Before Lucifer's rebellion, there was no concept of evil, so how could we possibly be sure what it was?

"It has to be about Lucifer's intent to rule," one of the others said.

I hunkered down a little more and tried to imagine what I would do right that minute had I been in Lucifer's place. I would be apologizing, groveling on the floor, and working on a plea. To this day I don't know why Lucifer risked it. He must have known he had picked a fight he could not possibly win. He should have backed down. That's what I would have done. The accusations against Lucifer began among the still kneeling, anxious angels.

"Why did we let him get this far?"

"Why wasn't his position enough?"

"Lucifer was cherished and denied nothing. Now look at what he's done?"

"He shouldn't have involved us. We haven't done anything."

"We're guilty by association; that's all. We don't deserve any punishment."

The angel next to me tugged on my wing and asked, "What did God think was going to happen? Is He going to take some responsibility for this?"

"What are you saying?"

"He spoiled him, overindulged his every whim. This really is partly God's fault, you know."

"God's fault?" I was unnerved at the utterance, though I had privately thought the same thing.

"Didn't God know that if He gave us the ability to defy Him, it would only be a matter of time until one of us thought to try it?" By now others were finding their tongues.

"He must have known it would happen in the right circumstances. Maybe Lucifer was tricked. It could have been one of us," came a voice from behind.

I said nothing more but began to think about Lucifer's defense. It was a bad idea on God's part to put both power and free will into the same being. If there were a better control system of checks and balances, none of this would be happening.

Not that it matters now, but I believe that in the beginning Lucifer truly loved God, but somewhere along the way, his love turned inward and decayed into a yearning for a power that was denied him. It happened after Earth was hung in space. Lucifer rebelled against the boundaries he had been given concerning Earth, whatever those boundaries might have been.

That's the thing you need to know about God. He sets boundaries. But here is where it gets fuzzy. If we wanted to do so, we could cross the line we were not supposed to go beyond. How's that for mixed signals? Why would

God make us able to do something we were not allowed to do? I've never understood that about God.

It was obvious to me that Lucifer was in trouble because he had crossed some kind of boundary concerning Earth, though no one knew what it was. God, who created and loved him, must now do one of three things: move the boundary, indulge him, or destroy him. I could see that nobody was going to win this one.

All of heaven could feel the heaviness in God's voice when He confronted Lucifer. When the rest of us realized God's favorite was not getting a pass, we got really quiet and waited to see how he would respond. Lucifer was outraged.

"Objection! Out of order! There is no legal precedent for this. How can this be?" he demanded of God, the court, and anyone else who might be listening. His voice trailed off as he began muttering gibberish as if Yahweh would know what he was talking about. None of us did.

Lucifer shamelessly began to accuse God right there in front of us.

I shuddered at how far he went as he ranted against the goodness of God.

"You are an imposter, God. It is Your power and not Your love that brings about Your will." Lucifer bellowed to the heavenly host that Yahweh was not a God of love at all.

Then he turned toward us. "He is a God of manipulation who creates free will and then denies it." Lucifer tore his hair and stomped his feet. He contorted with rage. His eyes were filled with fire and hatred. Like one gone mad, he spun to confront the other archangels who stood at their posts.

"Listen to me," Lucifer sputtered, "or you're next. Can't you see what is happening? This jealous God cannot be trusted."

"What does he mean, we could be next?" someone whispered from the ranks. The angels looked at each other as if the thought of such a thing had never been in anyone's imagination. Lucifer did not miss the uneasy glances exchanged between them. He pressed in harder.

"None of you are safe. See how He will destroy anyone who does not obey His every whim. Why do you think He has turned against me? He is jealous of His own creation."

I raised my eyes carefully to look at Michael's face. How long would this tirade against the Most High God be allowed to continue? I didn't know what would happen next or which way I would run when it did.

Nobody tried to stop him, so Lucifer continued to make it worse. "Only I of all the heavenly host dare to speak the truth. The rest of you are cowards."

Lucifer drew his sword from his belt and brandished it about so furiously, some stepped back from him in fear of losing a wing. I found myself cringing at every swipe and secretly wondered why someone hadn't taken that thing away from him as a precaution. Weapons are a bad idea in a courtroom. I wondered whether the consequences of Lucifer's fit might fall on the rest of us.

I really blame God for not putting an end to the foolishness right there. If only He had, the whole thing would have been over before the court of angels began to divide. "Surely they aren't choosing sides?" I thought. "Who would choose to side with a deranged archangel and against the Most High God?"

If there was going to be a fight, I wanted to get away before it started. I began thinking about the consequences if I stood in the wrong place. Some of the host moved close behind Lucifer as he condemned the cherubim, God's holiest angels, for their obedience to God. He accused them of pretending that their allegiance to the Ancient of Days was based upon love when in truth they were terrified of His absolute power and demands for unquestioned loyalty.

Lucifer jeered at them. "This God you bow down to would rather destroy my beauty and cast me down than admit that the creation has become more desirable than the Creator." Lucifer blistered the air as he whirled about with the flaming sword, ranting like one gone completely mad. "I will raise my throne above the throne of this misguided God. Choose whom you will follow, or die."

My eyes were twitching in terror, but God did not blink. It seemed for a moment like He might not do anything. Confusion grew as the angels asked, "What if it's true?"

Some of the neutral angels listened and believed Lucifer's claims and moved toward his side. Now, here's something you need to know about him. He is the prince of lies, but he doesn't lie all the time. He has no qualms about taking something that *might* be true and concocting a believable and persuasive fabrication that is completely wrong.

Once you hear one of his exquisitely constructed part-truth lies, you will find yourself thinking about it. Pretty soon, you will be wondering how it *could* be true. That's what happened to me.

I'm ashamed to admit it, but I found myself seeing things from Lucifer's point of view. He brought up an extraordinarily important question with repercussions for everyone. If God were willing to expel the prince of the archangels, His favorite, what might He do to any of the rest of us if we displeased Him?

"Ridiculous," I said to myself. "It would not happen. It could not happen. The whole idea was preposterous."

My last nerve was about to unravel when I realized that sides were being chosen for a fight, and no one would be allowed to sit it out. I zigzagged back and forth across the room, fretting about where to stand. If

I stood with Michael's warriors and they lost, Lucifer would destroy me for disloyalty. I had that clearly figured out. If I stood with Lucifer's side—way in the back, of course—and they lost, Michael might simply overlook me since he never seemed to notice me before anyway. It was possible. It was at least worth a try.

Then Adonai stood up—a bad sign for us all. Standing meant judgment was about to be unleashed. The Son of God pronounced the sentence on Lucifer. "You corrupted your splendor by your sin. You corrupted My Father's glory by your ambition. Depart, and be cast down to Earth," His voice thundered.

I could barely take in what I was hearing. Lucifer cast out? Cast out to where? To what place is an archangel exiled?

"God can't really banish an archangel, can He?" whispered someone whom I could not identify.

"Of course not," I muttered to myself, but I did not convince myself in the least.

Lucifer so miscalculated the nature of God; he truly believed God would not—could not—destroy what He loved. I can look back and see why this strategy never had any possibility of working. Lucifer failed to take into account that the *holiness* of God was as great as His *love*. God would not allow His holiness to be profaned among His creation, even for the sake of His love.

At Adonai's command, Michael unleashed his powerful army as war broke out in heaven. Lucifer fought back with all of his power, and one-third of the heavenly host fought with him.

The offense within Lucifer blazed and consumed his heavenly nature. "Thrown out? Expelled from heaven? Cast from the presence of the One who created me? No!" he raged. "You will never do it."

But God most certainly did. The war in heaven was on.

Lucifer raged against the judgment of the Most High God and lost not only his place in heaven but also his name. He would no longer be called "Lucifer the light bearer." He would be called "Satan the accuser," because he accused God and the other angels who remained faithful to Him.

Following Michael's orders, Rafael, Ariel, Gabriel, and the other archangels brandished their flaming swords with great skill and precision. They seemed to grow taller, enormous even, right before our eyes as we actually diminished before them. I could feel myself shrinking and my wings wilting before their wrath. That's when I realized I had been standing in the wrong place.

"Oh, no." I protested, scurrying toward the other camp. "I didn't choose sides yet. I was thinking it over." But it was too late.

One of the rebellious angels forced a sword into my hands, and I swung the best I could but hit nothing. I knew I looked foolish. Suddenly the atmosphere became suffocating and heavy. It was as if someone had removed the pillars that held heaven in place and unleashed an invisible force upon us. We staggered under the weight of what we could not see. Pressed down, barely able to stand, we felt a strong wind that came from nowhere and from everywhere at once. We rolled back and forth as we lost our footing. I felt dizzy beyond description.

"Oh, no," I thought as I tried to find somewhere to sit and hold my head steady until it stopped spinning. "Ruah Ha Kadosh has entered the fight."

Trying hard to stay out of the path of the clashing swords, I stood up as best I could and looked around for Michael or Gabriel or anyone who might be in charge and who would help me. I planned to grovel and beg for mercy for a chance to correct my incredible lapse in judgment. I threw the sword down and stumbled all over myself, getting to the rock where I hid until Michael came and cut off Damon's head. As Michael turned away, I shook my feathers out, rolled the dead demon's head off my foot, and practiced saying the words I would use to explain what happened. I would say how I had been standing in the wrong place and inadvertently appeared to be following Lucifer. I would crawl on my knees to Michael. I would explain how I'd been confused lately and frequently had trouble making important decisions.

Now, praise God, my mind had returned to me, but while it was gone, it appeared I had joined the wrong side of the war, which I never intended to do. When I realized my mistake, I fully repented and came over to the righteous side where I'd always intended to be before my mind left.

I could almost touch the hem of His garment. But I was not fast enough or close enough. Before I could offer a single word of repentance, with a mighty gush of breath, Ruah Ha Kadosh executed the word of God. Satan and one-third of the heavenly host were cast out of heaven and thrown to Earth.

Sadly, I fell with them.

CHAPTER 5

THE SENSATION OF falling was terrifying. We
flailed about like unstrung puppets caught in a
hurricane. We had no control over our movement and no frame of reference for what was happening.
We tumbled out of the realm of the heavenly light into
perpetual darkness unlike anything we had seen before—
not like this anyway. We had known the absence of light,
but we did not know that there could be such a pulsating
void of suffocating nothingness. We were falling through
a realm where the gloom was so thick that it could be
felt. It was a terrifying and strange place, and yet there
was something eerily familiar about it.

It was like an odor one has smelled before but now
cannot quite remember where or when. We had not realized that we were careening through second heaven,
which existed far below third heaven, where we had

lived with God. We didn't have long to ponder what this dominion might be like, because we continued to fall until we crashed through another border and reached another realm. When we regained our equilibrium, we knew that we had arrived on Earth.

Perhaps you wonder, "Why Earth?" Surely there were other planets more suitable as a penal colony for our rebellion. Planets where there was no life—desolate, barren, frozen, or parched. Surely Earth had not been created for us. Satan certainly knew about Earth. After all, he had longed to be given special charge over its affairs, but now, it was his prison.

I can tell you I realized right away our fate could have been much worse. At first one might argue that this was hardly banishment. Earth was more beautiful in those days than it is now. This fragile and delicate planet hanging alone in space had obviously been created for something important. It was not designed for rebels like us. Satan never really valued the beauty of Earth anyway, so its exquisiteness was completely wasted on him. From the day it was made, all of heaven knew how much God particularly favored Earth. So when I realized where we were, I thought there had been some mistake.

None of it made sense. Why were we alive? Why had we not been utterly destroyed as lawbreakers? What would we do on the most beautiful of the worlds God had created?

"Is this really Earth?" we asked each other.

"It must be," someone responded. "This is not so bad."

The others agreed; it could have been much worse. We could have landed on one of those horrendously hot planets.

"Must have been a mistake," someone else offered.

None of us had an answer, but I knew God did not make mistakes. We were here for a purpose, but only He knew what it was.

We wandered aimlessly about Earth for several days— I don't know how many. We were still outside the realm of time, so it was hard to know how long we had been there. While the others were arguing over territory, I found myself thinking about God.

How was He feeling about those of us who had betrayed Him? He had certainly loved us. I wondered if He missed us at all. As much as He loved us, we all felt that He loved Lucifer even more. We never knew whether it was true, but in the end, we didn't really mind. I've often wondered whether or not God ceased to love him because he behaved like an overindulged child. Did his rebellion truly change the affection of God toward him—or us for that matter? After all, God is so above the presumption and foolishness of His petulant creation. I wondered if God regretted His decision to cast us out without giving us a second chance.

No longer the light bearer of heaven, Satan the accuser and we whom he had mesmerized tried to figure out why we were on Earth. Satan really seemed to be as perplexed about it as the rest of us. Although, of course, he would never say so.

I also found myself thinking about the host who had remained in heaven and wondered if they were watching us. We used to do things like that, you know. We would stand on the edge of heaven and speculate about Earth. Knowing the angelic realm as I do and the angels' penchant for gossip, I could just imagine what they might be talking about.

"Why didn't Yahweh destroy the rebels?" they must have mused.

That's what I would have been asking. It's too simple to say that it was because God loved us so much He could not bear to destroy us. No one who knew the slightest thing about His holiness would consider such sentimentality. Perhaps simply being cast from His presence satisfied the demand of His holiness and His justice, but I doubted it. There had to be another reason.

Now as I look back on how things turned out, I wonder whether or not God regretted that He had not destroyed us right then and been done with it. Why didn't He use His might, indignation, strength, and power to utterly crush Satan and the rest of us? If He had, no one would have thought twice about His right to do so. He should have completely eradicated any memory of us. I daresay no one in heaven or on Earth would know that we had existed. It would have been as though we never *were* at all. Heaven could have gone on carrying out God's ideas like we never happened. We would have been obliterated from its history. No one would have known or wondered about us. If you ask me, God missed a fantastic opportunity to clean the whole mess up and be done with it.

Instead of ending it neatly and completely, as He probably would have if He had only thought it through a little more, God permitted the righteous anger in Michael to rise up. There was no doubt about who the players were. Michael and his angels utterly conquered us and drove us out of heaven.

"Is this Michael's fight?" the gossiping angels must have asked one another. "Why doesn't God seize the moment to demonstrate His omnipotence?"

Certainly the heavenly host was aware that the weight of His glory could destroy anything that opposed it. If you ask me, God left Himself wide open for unhealthy speculation among the remaining angels when He let Michael take the credit for the war. The utter destruction of the rebels by His hand would have forevermore insured that there would be no further rebellions. Why did He not show Himself forth in His unlimited might and authority? He must have known how history would record that it was Michael and his angels who overcame Satan. Was God even a little worried that this might go to Michael's head? After all, if Satan could be corrupted, then no one was exempt.

Perhaps it was because the power of God was never in doubt. I suppose He did not consider it necessary to demonstrate a power of which every one of us was certain.

At first I could not see why it seemed more important to prove His restraint and compassion where we were concerned rather than settling once and for all what could happen to anyone who thought he could outwrestle God. It took me awhile, but I think I finally figured it out. God would allow Satan to show the futility of existence apart from His presence. Heaven was watching, and heaven would learn.

If it were possible that a created being should have been able to muster his gifts and abilities (which Satan was permitted to retain) to be victorious, independent from God's presence, surely Satan was that one who could do it. And if Satan could do it, then others, as we had done, would follow. I thought God was taking a big risk to allow Satan the opportunity to realize his ambitions. He was given domain to rule just as he wanted. With no strings attached, this rebellious angel would be allowed to rule apart from the presence of the One who had created him. He would be permitted to establish his own throne and his own kingdom, but not in the heaven where God was.

All of heaven would be standing by, watching to see what he would do. With all of our powers and abilities and corrupted nobility, we found ourselves in a beautiful place crafted by the very hand of God but with no idea as to why. Having no further recourse to God and not willing to challenge him for control, we pledged our allegiance to Satan the accuser of our brethren.

But we did not pledge our devotion. We had known devotion only to God. We pledged allegiance to Satan out of fear and a lust for his power. We never doubted for a moment that Satan loved anything but himself.

I knew that all of heaven would be standing on the edge of eternity to watch and see what Satan would do with unrestrained power.

I could have told them.

CHAPTER 6

I WONDER IF IT is possible for the human mind to understand the horror of banishment. I doubt it. Perhaps you could try to imagine what it would be like to be suddenly disowned and thrust from Earth into space and sentenced to remain alive forever on another planet. How long would it take before the awareness of total abandonment and separation from everything that caused you to be who and what you are began to birth sheer terror into your very soul? It is not death, but it is everything you fear death to be.

I have observed human ways for a very long time, and I marvel at the extremes to which you people will resort to avoid death. It's not the idea of being dead that troubles you. Some might find death to be a welcome escape if only one could be assured that it were nothing more than an endless, dreamless sleep. As a matter of fact, even to me the notion doesn't seem that bad. What people fear about death is that it is nothing like that at all. You fear being awakened, regaining consciousness, and realizing there's been a terrible mistake: you're not dead at all. You're still alive but far removed from your home and familiar surroundings and cast into another dimension where you are entirely alone.

You fear death because the unthinkable hides in your imagination. What if death is only a door through which you are forced to pass, only to find that you have remained exactly the same person? You retain your consciousness, your talents, ambition, emotions, and every aspect of aliveness that gives meaning to your existence. But the world in which these things have meaning and relationship is suddenly closed off to you.

Your life on Earth was worthwhile only in so much as it had purpose, definition, and meaning to the world around you. You pass through the door called death, and the world you have known is gone. Your meaning and purpose are gone. There is no longer the possibility of a God to whom you can cry out. You are completely alone.

It was something like that for us to find ourselves suddenly on Earth with no way to return. We were angels, more glorious than you can possibly imagine and created to live eternally in heaven, not on Earth, no matter how pretty it was.

When I came to my senses after the crash, I was appalled at what had happened to Satan. At first I wasn't sure it was really him. How could he change so drastically? He was no longer the light bearer—or anything close to it. He was ghastly. The grandness of all that he had been was horribly changed. The light that emanated from him was completely gone. He was gray and thin— so thin I could almost see right through him. It became so apparent that his beauty and glory had only been real because of his relationship to God. His beauty, talent, and charm were real and meaningful only as he reflected the attributes of the God who made him. Disconnected from God, He became unspeakably ugly.

How can I explain the change in him? Imagine a Christmas tree decorated with ornaments and set aglow by hundreds of lights. You behold the beautiful tree in its halo of lights and exclaim how glorious it is. You don't take notice that its brilliance is completely dependent upon the hidden electric cord that winds itself silently from bulb to bulb until it is at last plugged into the electrical outlet where the power is. You don't become aware of it until the cord is unplugged and the tree becomes suddenly dark and loses its beauty. The ornaments are still there, as are the light bulbs and sockets, but the glory that is a Christmas tree is gone. That tree once so admired and set in a place of honor to be the center of your home is suddenly lifeless, dull, and dry. What was once a Christmas tree, full of promise, is now only a dead plant with meaningless ornaments and fake icicles that are too much trouble to remove. I have watched as you dragged it to the curb to be carried off by the garbage truck.

It was like that for Satan. All of the ornaments and reminders of his existence when he was the light bearer still hung on his being. But the relationship to God that had given him meaning and purpose was completely gone.

As it was for Satan, so it was for the rest of us who had fallen with him. It was stunning to see how our feet had become hooves. Even our wings were changed. Most of our beautiful feathers had been replaced with slimy scales. The others were like Satan, the essence of ugly. I had not found a way to look at myself, so I held out hope that somehow I might look a little better. In stunned disbelief at what had happened to us, we staggered about Earth as one who has consumed too much alcohol staggers about in his surroundings. He is not sure where he is. He is unsure of what has happened to cause such pain in his body. He is disoriented and tries to remember how he came to be in such a state. Yet at the same time, he is afraid to remember. Had he really done this to himself? Surely there was someone else to blame for his condition.

Regret and remorse are the most bitter of companions. At least that's how it was for me.

Once we realized the finality of this new reality, panic overtook our common sense, and we began to blame one another. Someone must be held responsible for what had happened to us. Finally, someone dared to say it.

"It was Satan's fault. He misled us."

"That's right. We would never have rebelled on our own," said someone else.

"How could we have been so foolish?" another added.

Then as one angry mob, they turned on him. I knew this to be an extraordinarily dangerous move. I knew they were underestimating Satan's wrath. I tried to tell them, but I couldn't get a word in, so I kept to the back of the group and waited to see which way things might go.

Of course, I was right, and things went bad quickly. I cannot begin to tell you what an ill-conceived idea it was to try to overthrow Satan. God had not destroyed us, but Satan almost did. Everyone had underestimated his strength, his power, and his capacity for ruthlessness. He obliterated the first line of attack against him, and I'm quite sure he would have annihilated the rest of us had it not been for one thing. We were all he had left. Whatever he planned to do, he would need us to carry it out. Make no mistake; we would remain alive only as long as he had use for us.

When we realized we could not match him in strength or power, we did the next most illogical thing.

We turned on each other. Well, everyone except for me. I hid behind a tree. As if we hadn't learned one thing from the futility of the war in heaven, we proceeded to wage war on Earth. If I could not fight in heaven, where I knew my way around, then I surely wasn't about to chance getting hurt and lost on Earth, having no idea where anything was.

They raged and fought against one another in an attempt to secure a position near Satan. After the failed coup, each one was anxious to prove a newfound loyalty to the fallen prince. I suppose they thought being near him might be the best place for protection, though protection against what, I don't know, since there was nothing on Earth more fearsome than them. Perhaps they thought Satan would reward those who were the closest to him. I think some naïvely held out the hope that Satan might rule them like God had. Not a chance.

I've concluded that angels, in their natural state, are not strategic thinkers. Perhaps it was because in heaven we never needed to evaluate cause and effect. God caused all things, and the effect was never in question. I'm pretty sure it never crossed anyone's mind that if they destroyed Earth, there would be absolutely no place for us to go. I thought about pointing it out, but I changed my mind. The enraged angels were intent on making things worse and looking for a target. It wasn't going to be me. Earth would have to fend for itself.

God's favorite planet reeled at the violence of the war between the fallen angels. As the human body reacts by spontaneously ejecting an object that can bring about its destruction, so Earth reacted to the devastation the warring angels wreaked upon it.

Earth itself began to fight back, but things only got worse. In their fury, rage, and horror at God and at each other, the angels unleashed their devastating powers upon Earth, never mind they were about to destroy the only place left for us to exist. The angry angels tortured and ravaged every beautiful thing God had placed upon this planet. All that did not perish immediately became defiled, injured, and hostile.

It seemed as though Earth had lost its balance, as the seas boiled from the pollution of the raging angels. The waters were black and ominous and began to overtake the land as if trying to escape its domain. Finally, the dark water overtook and drowned every point of light and beauty on the injured planet. That was the first flood upon Earth. It was Lucifer's flood, caused by his wrath, and it destroyed all the wonder God had created on this delicate blue and green bauble.

Earth could take no more. It jolted and spun off its course. It reeled and retched until it expelled us completely. It was as if we had been vomited from the mouth of Earth into yet another realm far above its surface. I knew we were in danger of being forever flung into nothingness. I thought we should apologize to Earth, make up with it if you know what I mean.

"Look, this could work," I told the others as we hung temporarily suspended between the planet and oblivion. "We can adapt and live sensibly upon Earth."

"And do what? Exist in the floodwaters? Nothing else is left," someone pointed out.

That's when Satan had his second bad idea.

"We will make our way back to heaven," he said as he began flapping his wings in an attempt to get traction.

"Why didn't we think of that?" came a facetious voice that could not be identified. "I'm sure God has gotten over the rebellion by now."

Futile as it was, we decided to try it. Everyone flapped for all he was worth. Some climbed on top of each other, as if getting tall enough would enable us to reach something. Satan climbed on top of everyone else, then he and some of the other strong ones were able to lift off and get a foothold into the kingdom of the air: second heaven. It was the same realm through which we had fallen when we were thrown out. It was not third heaven, mind you, or anything remotely close to it. It was dark and empty of all the glory that heaven is. It was a discarded part of eternity, but eternity nonetheless.

"This is close enough," Satan announced.

No one was going to argue. We knew if by some miracle we had made it all the way back to third heaven, the angelic guard would have been waiting for us, and who knew what might happen to us then?

That's how Satan's kingdom came to be established in second heaven. It was terrible. It was dank and cold. It would be some time before I learned that the awful smell was sulfa. Because God made all things, He must have made this place as well, but I couldn't imagine why. Since we had fallen through it when we were cast out, I knew it hung somewhere between third heaven and Earth. We had been able to climb from Earth to this place, so I wondered if there might be a back door leading to third heaven. I desperately searched for one but did not find it. An ironlike ceiling above and floor below contained this new abode. It had three closed sides like a cave and a ledge from which we could see Earth and the emptiness of space.

That's when Satan decided he needed an army.

"What will he do with an army?" I said to myself. "We lost the war in heaven, and we lost the fight with Earth. What else is there?"

I suppose he was looking for something else to attack, so an army it was, and, of course, a pecking order had to be established. He assigned us our place according to our aspects, which are particular talents held by some and not others. I didn't know exactly what kind of assignment I would have, but I was pretty sure it would be out of everyone else's way.

Satan declared that we were now an army of demons whose purpose was to serve him. That's what we were now—demons. Don't ask me why. We had become more like a street gang than a heavenly host.

The strongest ones he divided into categories of powers, princes, thrones, and principalities. Satan stirred them up by telling them they would have their revenge and rule again over Earth in due time. I was assigned to be the watcher with no real authority over anything. My job was to watch Earth and report what I saw.

"Total waste of time," I would have told him if he'd asked me, which he didn't. Satan couldn't seem to get a grip on the fact that he had lost Earth. If he wanted me to watch it, then watch it I would. I found myself a rocky perch on the edge of second heaven, where I set up my post.

The first thing I noticed was that some who had fallen with us were unable to rise above the chaos to reach the kingdom of the air. Some were too weak. They were more like angel-ettes, created without the multidimensions given to the stronger angels. Their personalities were limited to only one aspect, which made them, more correctly, spirits, not angels.

The spirits were created by God to be rapid messengers to carry out His will in heaven. Each spirit had been fashioned with an aspect of the nature of the Lord. I don't know why they were on Earth at all. They were not equipped with the same personality complexities that would have allowed them to choose to follow anyone, especially Satan. But there they were: cast-offs of heaven and now trapped on Earth. My guess is they were cast out with the rest for the same reason as me. They were probably standing in the wrong place at the wrong moment and got swept up in the hullabaloo.

When in heaven, a spirit was a useful delivery system for God. They could be dispatched quickly from His throne to impart His aspect, something of the nature of the Lord, when and where it was needed in any part of the universe. These spirits were named according to their purpose. One was a spirit of peace; another, a spirit of joy; yet another was a spirit of love. They would race to and fro and carry the aspect of God's nature wherever a piece of God needed to be. Their purpose was good and noble.

In one way the spirits were like me: never intended for battle. Battered and beaten, they were trampled upon by the stronger demons in the hasty retreat from Earth. The spirits were sacrificed and used as shields, hostages, and steppingstones by the raging demonic angels.

I could see they were in terrible condition. Their aspects were damaged and distorted. The angel who had once been Peace became Fear. Love became Hate. Joy became Despair. When they realized they had been abandoned on Earth, they panicked. By itself, a spirit with only one aspect would be at the mercy of any entity that could do more than one thing at a time. Left alone upon Earth they quickly learned they must cluster together to survive. Each groped about for another spirit with whom he could unite for protection, though against what I'm sure they did not know.

"We are cut off. We are cut off," they wailed as they realized there was no escape from the dank floodwaters suffocating Earth.

They sought one another out and clung to each other. Rejection and Fear of Abandonment would stay together. Envy, Greed, and Lust would hover together. Abuse, Anger, and Violence would enable one another. Shame, Self-Loathing, and Sexual Dysfunction would hide together in the shadows. They agonized, not knowing if they would remain in captivity to the angry sea or simply cease to exist. There was nowhere for them to hide, no vehicle, no habitation in which their aspects could function. They wailed and sank deep into the angry waters to which they had been abandoned.

They did not know a worse fate awaited them.

CHAPTER 7

FROM MY PERCH I was able to see the entire planet at one time. I had not fully realized the extent of the devastation, but now I could see how terrible it really was. It had been so beautiful and full of light and color before we arrived. But now, it was a catastrophe: dark, void, and empty; covered by Lucifer's flood; and nothing at all like it was when God made it. I wondered if He had the heart to look at what it had become.

The battered Earth was exhibit A in proving that Satan's rule did not include creating or preserving anything. The delicate blue planet in space was now nothing more than a swamp. Really, that is what it looked like. The whole place was little more than a cesspool where nothing but the formless spirits tried to hide. The dark waters churned savagely with the flailing about of the frantic phantoms fighting desperately to escape their watery prison. The dank and the dark covered the face of Earth. Nothing was left.

That is why I couldn't figure out Satan's continued obsession with it. Not a day passed when he didn't grill me about what was happening on Earth.

"Nothing is happening," I said. "Let me watch something else for a little while."

"No," he replied. "Let nothing escape your watch."

You know, you can look at swamp water for just so long before your mind starts to wander. Mine wandered off more than it should, especially when I would think about the unfairness of why I was condemned to such monotony in the first place. I wondered how I could go about appealing my sentence. Since no one was around, no one heard me calling to God and insisting that He review the evidence against me. He could have heard me if He wanted to. He sees and hears everything that happens in the universe, no matter how slight it might be. He didn't hear because He had dismissed me. I was a closed case as far as He was concerned.

The more tedious it became watching nothing happen on Earth, the more I forgot to watch at all. I spent my time thinking about my case and what I would say if I got a hearing in God's court. Fortunately, on that particular day I had collected my wits, was in possession of most of my mind, and was doing the job to which I been assigned: watching Earth do nothing. If I had as much as blinked an eyelash (which I really don't have), the whole thing would have escaped my notice. It was that fast. Something was happening in the water.

When I think how easily I could have missed it, I shudder at what the consequences would have been. It was so small, if I had looked away for a moment, I might not have seen it at all.

What I saw *happen* was in actuality what I saw *not* happening. There in the deepest part of the sea-turned-swamp, where the water had churned continuously for as many eons as I had been on guard, in a space no bigger than a clenched human fist, the water had stopped its relentless roil. It was perfectly calm.

"Now what do you suppose is causing that?" I asked myself. I stood as tall as I could on my perch and strained to see if there was something strange in the water—at least stranger than the frantic spirits I knew to be in there. How one understands "strange" is relative to his neighborhood. I blinked hard, then looked one more time.

There was no doubt about it. The calm spot began to ripple out and was growing in size at an alarming speed. At the same time the center from where it began became clear. My thoughts were running in a dozen different directions. I was really sorry I had left them unbridled for so long. I tried to gather them in long enough to formulate a coherent response to a rapidly changing reality. All the while the mirrorlike phenomenon was spreading quickly over the enlarging calmness.

I wondered what I should do. Should I report it? How would I explain it?

"Lord Satan, I wish to report nothing happening in the center of the sea."

I would have to do better than that, so I strained to look more closely. I tried to remember the cleanup operations I had seen, but I could not think of a single one that could cause those dank waters to become clear. The truth is, I could have flown out there for a better look, but I couldn't get myself going. There was something out there that caused what few remaining feathers I had to stand on end, and I couldn't do a thing with them.

At first it was hard to look, but then I could not look away. I knew I had to run or fly to tell one of the others what was happening, but I could get neither a foot nor a feather to cooperate. I flapped for all I was worth without going anywhere. Flying is not as easy as you might think, even for an angel. It requires a good deal of concentration. For example, if you only get one wing to flap, you can't really go anywhere, so you end up hopping around in a circle looking ridiculous. By now my concentration had shattered into little pieces, each locked on thousands of gently rolling waves, one after the other, full of clear water subduing the dark waters that had been there only moments before. The crashing anger of the sea was settling down as if it had become a gigantic pond.

"It cannot be. It cannot be." I must have said it to myself a dozen times. I gave up flapping and hopping and just stood there for a moment, completely mesmerized and undone by the miracle taking place before me and wondering how I was going to find the nerve to tell Satan that his nightmare had arrived.

Ruah Ha Kadosh was hovering over the waters of Earth.

CHAPTER 8

H UMANS HAVE NO concept of true fear. I have watched and listened to you for centuries as you speak of being afraid, as if you understood the meaning of the word.

"I'm afraid of heights. I'm afraid of the dark. I'm afraid of sickness. I'm afraid of being alone."

Humanity in its entirety consists of whiners—always has. How is it you humans have never understood that what you call "fear" is a warning system that God set within you for your protection? You fear heights, and so you do not teeter recklessly on the edge of a high cliff. You fear the dark, which experientially if no other way you must know is total nonsense. The dark is no match for the weakest human being. No matter the depth of the blackness, when a human appears with the smallest glimmer of light, do you people not see how the darkness flees?

You fear sickness, and so you take care of your physical bodies and disease has no entry point. You fear being alone and so are careful to behave in a civilized way so that others like you will want to be where you are.

This is not fear. It is a guidance system that God put within you to warn you when you are too close to areas of danger. Misunderstanding the point altogether and disliking the feeling you call fear, you humans take immediate action to alleviate the feeling. The fear you disdain is your protection, but most of you are too simpleminded to know it.

Shall I tell you about fear? I know it very well. When we first fell from heaven, only two of our emotions were in working order: fear and hatred. Some had so much hatred that they knew no fear. I was so afraid I didn't have the nerve to hate anything. I didn't know if our other emotions would ever function again. I wondered if I would miss the other feelings I used to know. We had them all, you know: love, joy, sorrow, sympathy, gratitude—all of them, same as you.

I especially missed sorrow. You likely cannot imagine what I mean since humanity exhausts itself trying to avoid feeling badly about anything. But I sometimes think that if I could only feel grief again, it would lessen the fear. If I could have conjured up a good cry, I just knew I'd feel better.

If only I could weep or feel remorse, perhaps that would hold the escalating terror within me in check. If I could feel one bit of compassion for the devastation we brought upon Earth, then perhaps the ravages of fear that consume me could be contained.

Here is how we differ, you and me. When you are afraid, you respond to the thing that is making you afraid. You turn on the light, move away from the edge, and take your medicine, and the fear subsides. You may even feel better than you did before the fear came upon you. When you do something about your fear, you overcome it and become its master.

Now here's how fear is an enigma for humans. The more fear you deal with, the less fear you have. Fear responds to humans in the same way that the darkness responds to humans. It knows humanity is its master. Fear knows that God has made it subordinate to mankind and that it must obey. It is so obvious. I marvel that you people can't figure it out.

It is not so with us. There is no limit to our capacity for fear. When we reach a new level of fear, that mark moves higher yet again. We can go deeper into fear, but we can never retreat from it. Do you wonder what we fear?

For the most part, we fear each other. We dare not break rank or our mutual destruction is assured. More than anything else, we fear Satan.

He's become much worse, you know. When we first fell, I really believe he was as confused as anyone else by what had happened. It took him some time before he realized our fallen condition was going to be eternal. As he processed that reality, his confusion lessened, and his hatred grew. His hatred is without repentance, and we worry his hatred will overcome his sense of survival, and if it did, he would unleash his wrath against us.

It is strange that we never feared God. Although His power was without limit, so much more so than Satan, He could have destroyed us with a glance, yet we never feared that He might do so. God's strength and omnipotence were never frightening to us. In fact, we were comforted by it because we knew He was our protector.

Not so with Satan. He would destroy us in a moment if it advanced his purpose the slightest bit. We know that. He doesn't do so because he needs us. He cannot carry out his horrible vengeance without us. Satan is not omnipresent, as God is. He cannot create, as God can. If he destroys one of us, he has diminished his army, and his army is all he has.

Nonetheless, we know that if we fail him in our assignments, his rage will overtake his cunning, and he will destroy the one who failed him. We must be victorious in our assignments or be destroyed, and yet victory in our conquests does not relieve our fear in the least. Victory itself creates more fear in us, and of a far worse kind.

You probably think that when we were expelled from heaven, that was as bad as it could get for us. Perhaps you think we will be forever contained in a sort of spiritual limbo, occasionally interrupting the affairs of humans. Oh, that it could be that way. But no, we have a future just as you have. A terrible, terrible day awaits us, far worse than anything we have experienced before. The more victorious Satan is, the worse the judgment that awaits us.

As I trudged back to the place where Satan had set his throne, I don't know which I feared the most. Was it what I had seen happening over the seas? Or was it the fact that I would be the one who had to tell him? I knew I must tell Satan what I had witnessed out there: Ruah Ha Kadosh hovering over the wasteland that had become Earth. Somehow or another, this would end up being my fault. I just knew it.

"Lord Satan," I stammered.

He didn't acknowledge me with words, just a glare that meant I was bothering him.

"I have a report," I continued. He interrupted me before I could finish my sentence.

"What? Don't lie," he snapped.

"There's a disturbance on Earth." I paused to check out how he took the first part. So far, so good. I tried to select my words carefully. "Now, I could be wrong about this, but I'm almost certain, well, not that certain, but as certain as one could be without getting any closer, which I didn't. It looks as if…"

He slapped me out of my *careful* mode right into *blurt-it-all-out* mode.

"Ruah Ha Kadosh is hovering over Earth. End of report," and I fell to my knees.

At least he didn't take the time to swing at me again or to blame me for something that was not my fault. He spun around and sped off for the edge of second heaven.

"No, no, no," he bellowed, sideswiping any demon along the way who made the mistake of getting in his path.

He came to such a sudden stop that he almost flipped right over and off the edge. "No!" he screamed into the vastness of space. "You cannot have it, God. It is mine. Earth is mine. Leave it alone."

As he railed against God, the darkness over the earth began to swirl and dissipate. Things moved quickly after that. The rest of the demons raced behind Satan and stood near the edge to see what was going on. It was thrilling and horrifying at the same time. Not since we fell from heaven had we heard the voice of God, but there it was, perfectly clear as His words pierced the atmosphere, and we fell on our faces as if dead.

He said, "Let there be light," and there was light.

You cannot begin to imagine what it was like. Let me try to explain so that you can understand our mounting fear. Illumination beyond what any eyes could bear penetrated the darkness and banished it from the face of Earth. All of the misery, destruction, ignorance, sorrow, and wickedness that had made up the "darkness" started to disappear. It was not light as you have experienced it. It did not come from a star or fire. It came from God Himself. It was blinding, without shadow, and there was no hiding from it. It was painful to us. It was as if our entire being were one great eye that had been in total darkness now suddenly thrust into glaring sunlight. That is what it felt like, only worse. One can close an eye that has been assaulted by bright light, but there was nothing we could do to shield ourselves.

Satan howled as he slunk back, seeking refuge in the deeper darkness of second heaven. We pulled back into the blackest cave with him, trying to hide and waiting to see what God would do next.

Then God said, "Let there be sky between the waters to separate them."

Every one of us was transfixed and unable to move. I had forgotten what it was like to hear Him speak and bring order out of chaos with just His word. How can

I describe what it was like to hear His voice again? It was like delicate bells and peals of thunder all coming together in beauty and majesty.

Everything within me yearned to jump up and cry out to Him, "Here I am, God. Please take me back. Let me come home with You." Instead, I rolled into a ball and bit my tail so I could not speak. I could not chance it.

Then God said, "Let the water under the sky be gathered to one place, and let dry ground appear."

It wasn't so much that God was creating something that never existed before. It was more like He was calling Earth back into its original order before our fury had been unleashed upon it. Not being subject to time ourselves, I can't really say how long it took us to scandalize and pillage Earth into the travesty it became, but for Earth, it was a painful and slow process. Now God was speaking, and the elements of Earth came into perfect order before the words were completely out of His mouth. Seconds—that's all it took for Him to restore Earth and cancel everything Satan had done to it.

That's when it first occurred to me that this was a very strange thing for God to do. Think about it. What was the point? Why would He send Ruah Ha Kadosh to call the chaos back into order? Didn't God know that it would happen all over again? At least that would be the case if He allowed Satan to retain any access to Earth. Since He had not yet destroyed any of us, I presumed that He wouldn't. But it made no sense to me to restore Earth unless He planned to banish Satan once and for all. I wondered if He had really thought this through. I wasn't the only one perplexed by this strange action of God.

"Why is He fixing it?" a demon near the door of the cave asked.

"He must plan to destroy Satan—and us," someone else whispered.

"He can't. He won't. It isn't time." I was relieved that someone besides me could confirm that such an action would indeed be outside the rules.

"He must be planning to send Satan somewhere else—and us with him," the first demon replied.

I didn't dare contradict an already nervous demon, but I knew that wasn't going to happen. He sent Satan to Earth for a purpose, and although I couldn't figure out what it was, it had to be for some other reason than tearing the place to shreds. God must have a plan that included restoring Earth, but what could it be, and why now?

Unless God intended to confine Satan in some way from being able to engage Earth, He would have to know history would quickly repeat itself, and Earth would again be reduced to shambles. Satan doesn't improve with experience. He can't be rehabilitated. If Satan could not rule Earth without destroying it the first time, the second time would only be worse.

The more I thought about it, the less logical it seemed. The only possible explanation was the obvious one. God jumped the gun, simple as that. He got ahead of Himself. In His desire to see His favorite planet restored, He completely overlooked the fact that He had yet to deal definitively with Satan. So God went right on restoring as if everything were going to work out just fine.

Then God said, "Let the land produce vegetation: seed-bearing plants and trees on the land that bear fruit with seed in it." And, *poof*, just like that, it was there.

"That's a waste of time," said the demon with the best view. "What on Earth needs fruits and seeds?"

Good question. There was no living thing on Earth now, except for the plants that just popped into existence a few minutes ago.

Satan stood up and walked in silence to the edge of second heaven. Saying not a word, he stood there, staring at what was happening, as if anticipating something. But what? He knew God better than any of us. If anyone could make a good guess at what God might do, it would be Satan. We watched him carefully to see if his countenance betrayed his thoughts.

"Is he trembling?" someone whispered.

"Shut up," another hissed, slapping at the stupid one who dared say such a thing where Satan might over-hear it.

I dared not look at him directly, but curiosity got the better of me, and I had to chance a peek. I swear it was true. No doubt about it, he was trembling—not like I would be doing, of course. He did not convulse or hyper-ventilate, but there was definitely a quiver there. Satan afraid? But of what? What could be scarier than him? It couldn't be fear of God. God had sent no signals that He might be thinking about doing something to Satan at this point. The former prince of angels was almost pitiful as he shuddered and stood silently by, unable to prevent what he saw happening on Earth.

It was after God set the sun and moon in place and set the celestial clock for the passing of seasons that we finally realized He was indeed up to something. He was about to create some sort of life on Earth. Of course, that was the purpose of the vegetation.

I didn't know what God had in mind, but what-ever life He intended to make had better be a superior model to Satan. Otherwise, Satan would have it for lunch before the first season was over. All of us were thinking the same thing. We watched with curiosity as He filled the seas, the skies, and the garden with living things. It was lovely and all that but, so far, it was nothing Satan would care anything about.

Perhaps if I had paid more attention to God's words rather than being so caught up in watching Satan quake, I might have figured out what was about to take place. I should have remembered that every word God speaks means something. Each of His words "cause" and then there is an "effect." No exceptions. I had missed the importance of the small words because I had long forgotten how to listen to God's voice. The little words, had I been paying attention, contained the key that could have explained everything and at least given us a warning. I should have known better, but I had not practiced my listening skills since I was thrown out of paradise with the real rebels. A person gets rusty.

You can only understand what a paradigm-shifting big deal was about to occur if you first understand the concept of eternity.

Eternity "is." Everything in eternity is "now." There is no progression of chronological or linear time as humans understand it to be. And so, when God labeled His work as the "first day," "the second day," and so on, I thought nothing about it. None of us could have imagined what He was about to do with that new dimension I mentioned earlier, the one He called "time." Even if I had realized what He was doing, I would not have guessed that it had anything to do with us. Earth might be subject to time, but not angels—or demons. We could observe it, but we were outside its boundaries. We were eternal beings, after all.

There was no warning whatsoever. When the pillars started shaking and collapsing and the floor shifted under us, we still did not get it. Then there came a loud rushing sound that almost deafened us and sent us tumbling until I thought we were falling out of heaven all over again.

When the tossing and rumbling finally subsided, I wasn't sure where we were. It seemed as though we were still in second heaven, but something was drastically different. We might never have really figured it out on our own had Satan not whirled to face us with wrath and rage and fear spilling from his eyes and his mouth.

"We have been sucked into time," he growled.

And that is exactly what happened. God set a clock for us. He introduced time into eternity. Seconds, minutes, hours, and days passing and not returning and not repeating. It was undeniable that we were being pulled forward in time, but toward what?

How can I describe it so that you can understand? Consider how you and everything upon Earth are subject to a law, a force that you know as gravity. It is a consistent and unchanging law that God ordained. You do not think about it because it has always been there. It is everywhere, and all things on Earth or coming near

Earth are subject to the law of gravity and will obey it—except for us.

We angels cannot see the force per se, although we can easily observe what it does, but we ourselves are not subject to its effect. There is no up or down for us; we just "are." If we were suddenly made subject to gravitational pull, it would be an unnatural shift in our sense of being. It would mean that we were part of Earth's destiny. It would mean that we had become anchored to its purpose. We would be forced to adjust to a new reality. For one thing, we would have to learn the limitations of direction.

Time had begun for us. Time was moving forward, and it was pulling us along. If it had "begun," did that mean it would also "end"? I had a million questions and no one to ask. What was the purpose of time where we were concerned? What could it possibly mean?

The others staggered about, each trying to find his equilibrium in this strange new reality, so no one was interested in discussing the philosophy of it with me.

Perhaps it is because we now had a reference point in time that what happened next seemed so startling. If it had occurred in heaven, third heaven where God lived, it would have been ordinary. No one would have noticed.

After all, they were always together in paradise. The three of Them—Yahweh, Adonai, and Ruah Ha Kadosh—the Godhead. But suddenly, there They were on Earth. I was sure we had never known them to leave heaven.

"What is happening?" the demon voices murmured to each other.

"Look, there!" another voice shouted.

We looked up and saw Michael's warring angels gathered at the perimeter of this new expanse called "sky." I just knew they were there to hunt us down and finish us off.

"Run, run, run," I stammered pulling on the wings of the demons, trying to make them see the good sense of getting away. One brushed me away so hard that I lost my balance and fell, where I decided to stay. Looking through the group of standing demons, I could see the mighty guards of heaven with their fiery swords drawn and at the ready, but for what purpose if not to wipe us out?

Suddenly, everything and everyone became eerily still. A reverent silence descended around us. It was as if everything in heaven and Earth had stopped for a moment—even time. The winds pulled back in complete stillness. No sound interrupted the unmistakable sanctity of the moment. Something unprecedented was about to happen on Earth. I myself had chills.

Satan knew it also, and he paced back and forth feverishly trying to anticipate what the Holy Trinity was about to do. I had to see what was going on, so I convinced myself the warring angels weren't interested in me, and I slowly stood and joined the others. I could see the Holy Trinity clearly as they moved together as in a dance over the surface of the newly restored planet. In such perfect harmony, it was difficult to be sure who was doing what, but I dared not go any closer. Ruah Ha Kadosh hovered as Yahweh (or was it Adonai? I cannot be certain—it was just God) stood upon the face of Earth.

Then God said, "Let Us make mankind exactly in our image, male and female. Let them rule over the fish of the sea and the birds of the air, over the livestock, over all the earth, and over all the creatures that move along the ground."

It was impossible to distinguish among them as the Trinity. God touched the earth, scooped mud into His hands, and spat into it, forming a kind of clay. Right there in front of us He made a human being and named him Adam. Then, Yahweh or Adonai or both—what does it matter anyway—kissed Adam, and Ruah Ha Kadosh entered his nostrils, and Adam came to life.

CHAPTER 9

I WILL CONFESS TO being stunned by Adam's appearance. He was the spitting image of God, if you will pardon the pun. There was only one of him (we wouldn't figure out the male and female part until later), and beyond a doubt, he encompassed the essence of the triune God. I believe that may have been the moment when Satan slipped over the edge into complete madness. There is no other explanation for his behavior. His wrath exploded into bleating howls that he bawled and growled into the expanse above as he threw aside every demon unfortunate enough to be near him.

At the time, I could not think of any reason for such unrestrained rage. "No, God!" Satan spewed the words as he burst out from the edge of second heaven. "This creature will not have You."

tan was behaving like a scorned lover who was bent destroying not only a rival but also himself in the process.

With nary a thought to the consequences, and fueled with passion and jealousy, Satan flew with force toward Adam to destroy him. In less time than a flash can occur, Michael and the warring angels descended around Adam with their swords drawn for battle and the certainty of victory on their faces. I was scared half to death, but I don't think Adam had a clue as to the danger he was in. He stood there not appreciating the scale of warfare about to breakout over him.

Of course Satan could not pass the angelic line of defense. As he drew near them and saw their flaming swords, he came to his senses and realized they would destroy him with pleasure. They only needed an excuse. The bruised archdemon regained his sense of self-preservation and whimpered back out of their reach. We dropped our gaze to the ground and pretended not to have seen anything.

He should have known Michael would stop him. Maybe his jealous fit had short-circuited his thought-processing ability. That might explain some of his faulty reasoning. Because he had once held a position of authority in heaven, perhaps he thought he still had influence where the angelic guard was concerned. Of course, it was not remotely true. Although he ruled over us, fallen as we were, he retained nothing of the majesty and power of the faithful angels. Compared to them, Satan had become, well, *wimpy* is a good word (although, please, don't attribute it to me). The heavenly host could have destroyed him easily. I wondered why they didn't just go ahead and get it over with.

Humiliated to his core, Satan limped back to the precipice of our domain and glared at those of us who had witnessed his meltdown. We stretched our wings, shuffled our hooves, hummed a little tune, and pretended like we hadn't seen a thing. We absolutely had not seen Satan rebuked and mortified by the warring legion of the heavenly army. As far as we were concerned, it never happened.

Like a child in a temper tantrum, Satan did everything but hold his breath and turn blue. With his claws clenched tightly together, he continued to watch what was happening upon Earth. Some of the other demons and myself moved away from where he stood, hoping his preoccupation with Earth would prevent him from hearing us.

"Did you see what happened back there?" the first demon ventured.

"Did you see how he reacted to that clay man God made?"

"Why couldn't we have seen this earlier?" another asked.

"If we had, none of us would be here now. It was embarrassing. He acted more like a spurned lover than the prince of power he calls himself," another voice interjected.

"It was a lie," another whispered. "God was never jealous of Satan. Satan was and is jealous of God's affection toward anyone else."

"I knew it all along," a voice came from the side.

"Knew what?" asked a chorus of voices.

"I knew about his jealousy for God. That's why he hated Adonai."

Gaping mouths and wide eyes is about all we could muster in response.

"What do you mean he hated Adonai?" several asked at once.

"Couldn't you see it when we were in heaven? No one was closer to the Father than Lucifer—Satan—except for the Son. Lucifer never wanted to be the Father; he wanted to be the Son. How could you not have seen it? It's always been about his jealousy of Adonai."

"But he said he would raise his throne above God's. We heard him say it," another demon reminded us.

"No. You assumed he meant Yahweh's throne. That was never the case. He wanted Adonai's throne."

I covered my ears with my wings and refused to listen to anything more. I knew I would never be good under Satan's intense questioning, and I didn't want him to pull such gossip out of me. I couldn't tell what I hadn't heard, and I'd already heard far more than I wanted to.

I knew it was dangerous, but I ventured back toward the edge of second heaven to get a closer look at how things were coming on Earth. What was this "mankind" that God had made? It probably meant something terrible for us; at least Satan thought so. Otherwise he wouldn't have had such a public fit about it.

Satan saw me as I started to slink away, but he insisted I stay on guard with him to hear and record every word God might speak to Adam. Of course, I obeyed, although most of what was going on with Adam was not that interesting. God had to tell him every little thing to do. This new life form couldn't figure out a thing for himself. It was boring for both of us, but then think about our frame of reference. Once a person has stood in heaven and watched God create universes and solar systems from nothing, watching a clay imitation of God name animals was not that exciting. But it wasn't long before things got a lot more intriguing.

God said to Adam, "Multiply and subdue Earth, and take dominion over every living thing upon it."

"Multiply?" I said aloud. "What does God mean by that?"

I puzzled over what God could have meant by such a strange command. Adam was not like the animals. He was much more like God Himself. They, the Trinity, do not multiply. They just *are*. I was very confused and wondered if Satan knew what He meant. Before I could ask the question, he grabbed me by my tail and swung me around till I was facing him. He yelled into my face so that I had to close my eyes at the heat from his words.

"Adam will not rule over anything. Earth is mine." He seethed at me as if daring me to disagree, which was the absolute last thing I intended to do. Oddly, Satan did not seem at all fascinated by the "multiply" idea but latched right on to the "rule over everything" part.

"This will not stand." He threatened, cursed, and paced, but he also knew the truth. As long as the warring angels stood guard around the sky's perimeter, watching over this new creation, Satan would not be able to come near Adam to see what he was about. It would be his certain destruction.

Bored with it all by now, Satan turned and trudged back toward his throne in the center of second heaven, and I tried to follow. Before he could get comfortable on his seat, the sound of a great rushing wind and a pillar of white fire appeared before him and split the darkness that had been his refuge. Satan grasped the arms of his throne and sat frozen in place.

I jumped backwards and wrapped myself around my perch and held on for all I was worth. I knew what was happening and who was making it happen, although I could not look upon Him. Ruah Ha Kadosh had opened the heavens, and there before us stood God, the Ancient of Days. He was magnificent. His hair was like wool, His eyes flame, and He roared over the heavens, the earth, and everything that was or would be. All of us except Satan collapsed before His splendor, unable to move and hoping to die quickly rather than face His wrath. The wrath of Satan cannot be spoken in the same language used to describe the wrath of the Ancient of Days.

"Where can I hide?" I cried before I got hold of myself and realized that there was nowhere to go to be out of His sight. Surely it would be over very soon. He would destroy us. I knew it.

Still wrapped around my perch, I tucked my tail under, shut my eyes, and waited to die. And still I waited. (This new time thing must not be working properly. Obviously it had stopped.) What was happening? Nothing.

I chewed on my tail to relieve the stress. Still nothing. I opened one eye. Yes, I was still present. My tail would never look the same, but I was still alive, which meant that Satan and the others must still be alive too. I dared not try to open my other eye because I could feel that the glory of God was still somewhere about.

Then the Ancient of Days spoke to Satan. "Do you see what I have made on Earth?" Satan did not respond.

The voice of God continued, "I have created Adam to redeem and restore what you have attempted to destroy.

They will reign with Us in the place that you coveted and lost by your rebellion."

Why did God keep referring to Adam as "they"? I wanted to ask someone, but I decided then was not a good time to bring it up.

Heaven and Earth hung suspended together as if in a fragile balance altogether, all at once and all at the same time. Physics would have to explain it; I could not. At first there was silence as Satan glared past God directly at Adam, who, in my opinion wasn't coming close to grasping the seriousness of this situation.

Satan found his voice and managed to growl out what I thought was a very good question. "What is this man that you are mindful of him? What has he done either good or bad that You would make him ruler over Earth?"

"This Earth is mine, and I will not give it up," he continued. "Will You steal it from me? Why don't You just destroy me now in the presence of witnesses? Show Yourself for the tyrant God that You are."

I did not expect God to answer at all, much less to answer as He did.

"Adam will obey Me, and they will accomplish all that I have purposed. I will love them with an everlasting love. They will love Me and follow Me completely."

Satan shot back, "They will not. If they have free will, they will not obey You. Will You leave the warring host to guard them so that their affection for You cannot be tested? That is no contest."

I desperately hoped Satan would stop talking. I didn't know how much more God was willing to take from this rebel.

"Is that what you call love?" he taunted God. "Let them freely choose between You and me. It will be as it was with the angels whom You despised because of their devotion to me. Adam will laugh at you. They will defy You. They will follow me. Unless you force them to obey, they will choose my ways over Yours. They will hand Earth back to me."

From where I crouched in fear, I could see both the angelic guard on the edge of the sky and the faces of the fallen demons who poked their heads out of hiding to hear how God might answer Satan's accusation. As I looked at the perplexed faces in both camps, I realized how much God was willing to risk on this untested prototype of humanity. Both sides had something to win or lose on the basis of how well Adam functioned.

God replied, "I have given Adam complete free will, just as I gave you. If they obey me, I will do all that they ask."

What was I hearing? I was so confused by what God said that I lost concentration, and I am uncertain what happened next. The blackness had returned, and the glory of God had departed. That much I knew, but it was all I knew.

It was not like God to make a wager, and yet that appeared to be what He did. He must be trying to make a point, but what could it possibly be? He was allowing a contest with consequences all of heaven would regard as unthinkable. If Satan had not obeyed God, why did God think that this much-inferior model—Adam—would or could obey?

When things settled down, I unwound myself and moved closer to the edge and looked down upon Earth. I wanted to get a better look at this race God had created. Adam was not that impressive. He had a physical body. That right there was the first mistake God made with him. How could Adam fight against a supernatural foe when he was confined to a body of flesh that could be injured, perhaps even destroyed? An obvious design flaw.

He did not seem to have any particular talent. He could not fly. I suppose he was beautiful, but hardly a match for any of us, at least how beautiful we used to be. His physical body had to be fed. It had to sleep, a concept I could not relate to, although I admit it did have a certain appeal for me. (From time to time I've actually closed my eyes and tried to do it, but I cannot seem to get the hang of it.)

Angry as I was at God for never giving me a chance to plead my case before Him, at that moment I felt sorry for Him. This was never going to work out as He hoped. That free will thing was the fatal flaw. I couldn't imagine Satan would take Adam seriously. I turned to leave when my eyes caught sight of my evil master staring at Adam. I shall never be able to erase from my memory the ghoulish thing I saw in his contorted face. He stood salivating after the man.

CHAPTER 10

SATAN WENT BACK to his den, and I returned to my post to watch Earth. I had to admit it was a lot more interesting now that it had been reordered and mankind created. I was curious to see how it would turn out.

God made a fabulous home for Adam in a garden personally designed for him. God named the garden Eden, and it was lush—full of every kind of tree and plant that would ever be needed by humans or animals.

There were many trees in Eden, but only two that mattered: the tree of life and the tree of the knowledge of good and evil. God told Adam, "You are free to eat from any tree in the garden, but you must not eat from the tree of the knowledge of good and evil. For when you eat of it, you will surely die."

Considering the consequences of the cosmic rebellion, surely someone in heaven must have tried, albeit unsuccessfully, to convince God that His insistence in giving Adam the ability to choose between one thing and another was a terrible idea that had no possibility of ending well. If God couldn't be talked out of the free will idea, He should have at least let Adam practice a little on something that had no consequences. Let him choose between an apple and a kumquat. Don't let a novice's first choice be one that could alter the balance of the whole world.

The choice to obey or not is far too dangerous to be experimented with. It should be banned from every universe. I could be the poster child for why free will is an eventual disaster for anyone who has it. The ability to defy God is the cause of all my misery. Lucifer decided he could rebel against God. One-third of the angels chose to follow Lucifer. And what did it gain for us? Loss of everything we once held dear—loss of our home with God; loss of our purpose for being; loss of our high place; nothing but loss with regret, despair, fear, and hatred becoming our destiny.

Why does God insist on imposing free will on creatures who cannot possibly use it correctly? He knows what is best for everything He creates. We would be so much better off if He just eliminated the choices. I would not be wasting my existence sitting on a perch in the service of a tyrant if God had only restricted Satan's ability to defy Him.

It is that part of God's nature I cannot understand. He created all there is and all there will be, and He made it perfect. Then, for no reason anyone can explain, He programmed in a fatal flaw. Into every intelligent life form, God deposited the ability to defy its Creator. Can someone help me understand why this was a good idea?

Believe me, I know the company line: God wants those who love Him to do so of their free will. He will coax. He will woo. He will implore. But He will not force His creation to obey, though He could easily do so. How much trouble would He have saved Himself and how much devastation and misery could have been avoided if the rebellion in heaven had never taken place?

I can attest to the fact that we who were cast out of heaven would be so much better off today if God were only willing to be a benevolent dictator. Suppose that we had not chosen to rebel because the choice was not available to us. What if we had been slaves in obedience to Him? Certainly we would still be in paradise and never have known the difference.

Then assume that we annoyed Him in some way and in His anger He cast us out of heaven anyway. If it had happened like that, we would be in the same place where we are right now. And yet, I daresay we would be so much better off. If our destiny would have been the same, what difference would it make *how* we were thrown out? I know I would feel better if I could blame this on God's will and not mine.

When God said He would give free will to Adam, I wanted to shout, "Don't do it, God! Look at us. Look at what it does to those who are less wise than You." But I dared not say a word. It would have been the end of me. When Satan realized that Adam would indeed have the ability to choose, his excitement at what this might mean could not be contained.

Adam's job description was not that hard. He was given ruling authority over the garden, and if he obeyed and worshiped God, he could count on living happily ever after. How hard was that? As I understood his assignment, Adam was to push the boundaries of the garden further and further into the unsettled land until Eden covered Earth. Should have been a piece of cake for someone created in the image of God.

That is very well how it might have ended up if God had not given Adam the option of choosing between those two trees. By far, that was God's worst mistake with Adam. But it wasn't His only one. Let me tell you about God's second greatest lapse in judgment.

CHAPTER 11

G OD DECIDED TO separate them.

She was always in there. I'm not sure why God kept her hidden at first, but whatever she was, she was not an afterthought. It may have been because Adam was an experiential learner. If God had surprised him with the concept of a partner before showing him what a partner was for, I'm pretty sure Adam would have missed the point entirely. God was always patient to walk him through the practical application of a great idea before turning him loose with it. God knew He had to lead Adam to the point of wanting a partner before springing the woman on him.

It was brilliant how God went about it. He gave the man the task of naming the animals. This meant he had to really look at the animals to know what they were before he named them. In doing this work, I believe that he immediately latched on to the comfort that two animals, male and female, provided for each other. It also allowed him to figure out there was no suitable partner for him among the animals. That may seem obvious, but in all honesty, Adam was not that quick on the uptake. It took him forever to name the animals. I thought he would never get around to broaching the subject with God, but one day he did. He asked for a partner.

Eager to give her to him, God told Adam to lie down and go to sleep. While he was sleeping, God took one of his ribs and then closed up the place with flesh. Out of that one bone, God revealed Eve. When Adam woke up, there she was, and she was gorgeous.

We angels were familiar with every living thing in the universe. We have seen about all there is that is beautiful, but I have to tell you, she was a showstopper. We were somewhat dazzled by this new creation. Until God took Eve out of Adam, we had never had a frame of reference for anything female. The angels were all male. Adam was male, or so we thought, but apparently not entirely. We couldn't figure out what she was for. She was like Adam, smaller though, but with a lot of upgraded features. I found myself strangely attracted to her, especially her long hair that flowed and shimmered like strands of gold. In terms of beauty, God really outdid Himself with Eve. Clearly, she had been part of Adam from the beginning, but now, she would be distinct from him. I wondered if that meant that she would also have free will.

They were amazing to watch. They loved and trusted one another right from the beginning. I suppose it might have been something like the affection and trust they held for God Himself. There was no envy, no struggle for power, no suspicion between them. The demons could have learned something about teamwork by watching them, but, of course, you cannot teach a demon anything.

The man and woman worked together at the task of the garden hand in hand, each helping and submitting to the other. Adam had more physical strength and wanted to protect her. Protect her from what I don't know, since we weren't allowed in the garden yet, but it was quaint to watch them. She did not seem to mind the difference in their body mass and his obviously greater physical ability.

I remembered how I once felt that way about God. I did not feel diminished because His power was so much greater than mine. At least, I didn't feel that way until Satan pointed it out to me. Between Adam and Eve there was intimacy and trust I had not seen since we lost paradise. Unfortunately for them, Satan saw it too. Naturally, that would be the first thing he would try to destroy.

As I watched them, I began to appreciate how God had created them equal but interdependent on one another.

Adam won out in the brawn category, but without a doubt, Eve was the thinker. Adam could do amazing things, but it was Eve who figured out what things were worth doing.

Had Eve never come along, the flaw in Adam's ability to communicate with another human might never have come to light. When God was the only person Adam had to talk with, it didn't matter that much how good he was at detail. After all, Adam could not possibly tell God something He did not already know. I'm certain God must have been aware of Adam's proclivity to speak in headlines: no paragraphs, no fine print, no sidebar articles. So why did God leave it to Adam to tell Eve what the rules were? Adam was sure to leave out something important.

Every evening God came down and walked through the garden with Adam and Eve. I listened carefully because Satan wanted a full report on every word. Each night, before the presence of God ascended from Eden, I would find myself wanting to call after Him.

"God, wait. Tell her about the rule. Tell her about the two trees. Don't leave it to Adam. It's Your only rule. He's sure to forget something."

Of course, I never did any such thing. I would not have dared, and God would not have listened.

As I knew would happen, the day came when Eve asked Adam about the two trees in the garden. I was afraid he would gloss over the importance of what God said about the trees and leave out some important detail. I worried about the wrong thing. He left nothing out. In fact, he added to it.

CHAPTER 12

S
ATAN BECAME POSITIVELY obsessed with the new dimension of time. It didn't mean much to the rest of us since we didn't feel its passing anyway. We might have forgotten about it completely were it not for the fact that Satan kept saying we hadn't much time or we would soon be running out of time. I wondered, how would one go about doing that? If we ran very fast, did it mean that we would run past it? And if we did, what of it? We had always been outside of time before.

He watched Adam and Eve intently now, studying their every move. I thought he might try to approach them soon after God's departure from the garden, but he didn't. He just watched them. He paid attention to everything they did. He shied away from his watching post in the evening when God appeared in the garden and walked its paths with the two of them. Satan did not want to be seen by God (as if line of sight were necessary for God to know what was taking place). He knew. He always knows.

We were surprised when Satan called us together to tell us his plan. He never consulted us about anything. I guess I'm not really sure he ever had plans before. He simply set about to do whatever was on his mind at the moment. He certainly never weighed consequences, nor was he concerned about what any of us might think. The fact that he was thinking this through and waiting, watching, and planning must certainly mean the stakes were high. Whatever his plan might be, it would be certain to include the destruction of Adam and Eve. Satan could never corule with anyone. We obediently lined up to hear what he had to say.

"I have a plan to reclaim Earth," Satan announced. "I will tempt Adam and Eve to disobey God."

The demons who were out of Satan's view rolled their eyes and nudged one another until the one at the end of the line ventured a response.

"Uh huh," he said. "Now that is an interesting idea."

More glances and firmer nudging until someone else dared comment.

"Has lord Satan thought about what it might take to tempt people who already have everything they could possibly want?"

That is exactly what I would have asked if I had the nerve. What could he possibly use to tempt someone who lived in a virtual paradise where they lacked nothing?

"I will convince them God has withheld something valuable and I alone can offer it," Satan smirked.

Murmurs of approval circulated among the demons. No one could guess what it might be that God had not provided, so it was a normal question when someone asked, "What is it you will offer them?"

In a serious voice, Satan responded, "I will tempt them with a piece of fruit."

I bent down, stuffed my hoof into my mouth, and bit down hard. "Chomp, bite, choke, swallow your hoof, but do not chortle. Do not even grin," I warned myself.

The murmuring and nudging started up again. Finally, the demon at the end of the line stepped forward and spoke up. "Fruit, is it? You're going to tempt them with fruit. I see, well that could work."

"That could work," echoed the other demons in mock approval.

"But I wonder, my lord," the demon continued, "did you notice that the garden is full of fruit trees? Of course I don't know anything about it, but fruit as an enticement to disobey God? Do you really think so, Master?" He groveled away before Satan could swing at him.

"Imbecile," Satan roared. "Of course, it is not ordinary fruit. I will offer them fruit from that which is forbidden to them—fruit from the tree of the knowledge of good and evil."

"They might be curious about it," I mused silently, "but that couldn't possibly be enough to entice them to defy their Creator. How good can fruit be?"

Satan must have been able to read the doubt on our faces when he said, "Watch and see what I will do."

Just that fast, he was flying toward Earth. We crowded up to the edge of second heaven. I was amazed when I saw what he was up to. I had no idea he could do such a thing. As easy as you please, Satan took on the form of a serpent right there at the entrance to Eden.

"Did you know he could shape-shift?" someone asked.

"I didn't know that," came the answer.

"Neither did I," said someone else.

I myself was stunned Satan could assume the form of some other living thing God had made. When could he have learned to do it? He'd been with us the whole time. Amazing! Just when you think you know a person. I must admit that it was very clever to choose an animal as beautiful as the serpent. I secretly wondered if any of the rest of us had such talent and couldn't wait for an opportunity to try it myself.

I realize that you have no idea how beautiful the serpent was when God made it. It walked upright and had arms and legs like many other animals. It did not have a forked tongue, nor was its bite poisonous. What the serpent was then and what it is now is an object lesson in why one does not want to be the object of God's curse.

We watched as the serpent positioned himself against the tree of the knowledge of good and evil, as if it were an ordinary tree. He made it look easy and safe. Nothing bad happened to him as he sat on a low-hanging branch and plucked a piece of fruit from it. His being able to do this was a critical marker as far as I was concerned. If Satan were able to come in contact with the tree with nothing happening to him, it seemed less likely there was any real danger for the humans either. I wondered why God had made this such a big deal.

Adam and Eve were both working in the garden that day. Satan waited until Adam was some distance away and then called out to Eve. When Eve saw him, she was completely disarmed by how comfortable he was languishing on the tree branch that held so much fear for her.

I think Satan intentionally waited until he could talk to Eve alone, out of earshot from Adam. There was no doubt he was fascinated by her beauty and how different she was from Adam. I must say she was captivating. After their separation into two beings, Satan rarely looked at Adam anymore. But I would often find him leaning over the edge of second heaven staring at Eve.

"Did God really say not to eat of this tree?" he asked.

Clever of him to do that. Satan did not really accuse God of anything right then, not taking the chance of putting her on the defensive. He merely asked a question. And a very good question it was. Then Adam returned to see what was going on, but he said nothing. He did not seem that concerned that the serpent was talking to Eve. After all, at that time all animals could talk. One of them was always talking to Eve, her being the much better conversationalist of the two. The animals lost their language after the curse, but I'm getting ahead of myself.

Ignoring Adam, who was distracted by a bee flitting about his head, the serpent jumped from the branch and sauntered around the trunk of the tree, pulling off some of its leaves to Eve's complete astonishment. In a soft voice, the serpent said to Eve again, "Did God tell you not to eat from this beautiful tree?"

"Yes. He said we could not eat from it or we would die."

"Now why would God say that? You can see it's harmless, can't you?" He reached for another ripe piece of fruit and extended his hand to offer it to Eve. Eve took a step back and gasped at such an action.

"No. We cannot eat the fruit. We cannot even touch the tree or we will die."

"Oh, no," I cried. "I knew it! I predicted this would happen!" I ranted in a rare display of emotion as I stomped back and forth behind the line of demons. "I knew Adam would never get it right! Why did God leave it to him to tell her about the rules of the trees?" The other demons had no idea what I was talking about and ignored me completely.

Adam, never one for detail, had obviously told Eve not to eat from or touch the tree. God said nothing about touching anything. One rule in the entire universe, and it gets misinterpreted in its very first use.

The serpent grinned and continued to dangle the fruit in front of Eve, who stepped further back, being careful not to accidentally brush up against the fruit. Adam reached out and took her by the arm.

"Uh, Eve," Adam found his voice. "I'm not sure that's what God said."

"What do you mean you're not sure?" she asked. "We are not to eat from the tree or even touch it. That *is* what God said, right?"

"He probably didn't say anything about touching," Adam said as he swatted at the bee.

"Adam, pay attention," said Eve as she grabbed his swatting hand and brought him face-to-face. "You need to be very sure about this."

"Yeah, yeah, well, I'm pretty sure. He didn't say anything about touching."

Eve turned away and looked like she might cry. Adam took her by the shoulders and gently turned her around.

"Don't be upset. So much was going on that day. I could have heard God wrong." Adam strained as if trying to remember as he looked at the serpent pulling leaves off the tree. "I guess God must not have said anything about touching, or the serpent would be dead."

Eve did not seem convinced. She said nothing in response and looked at the serpent sheepishly.

The serpent moved slowly toward her, saying, "The tree is right here in your garden. Why would God care if you ate from it or not?"

Both of them folded their arms, shifted their weight from foot to foot, and looked uncomfortably at each other, then at the serpent, but neither had an answer.

"There can only be one reason," said the serpent as he pulled off more leaves and crushed them between his fingers. "There's a power in the tree God doesn't want you to know about."

"What kind of power?" Adam asked.

"The power to know good and evil. If you eat the fruit from this tree, you will be like God. You will know everything and will never die."

Adam and Eve stepped away and whispered quietly with their backs to the serpent. I listened intently as they talked themselves right into what Satan had wanted them to believe all along: nothing was forbidden. If God had said it was forbidden, then He must have an ulterior motive. Very clever, indeed, I must say. They walked back to where the serpent was, and Eve extended her hand.

"Don't do it!" I shouted into the air, but I knew they were going to do it anyway. The other demons looked at me as if I were addled, but they weren't interested enough to find out why.

The serpent gave Eve the fruit; she took a bite and then gave it to Adam. I would come to be amazed, as history unfurled, how humans got the idea this was Eve's fault. I was there, watching and listening from the first day God gave the rule to Adam while Eve was still a rib. It had to be Adam who gave Eve the information about the tree. How could she have known any other way? No one else heard, so no one can be sure what he said to her.

Maybe Adam did it with good intentions. I've seen other humans do the same sort of thing when warning someone they care about of possible danger. I've heard them overstate the consequences without the slightest hesitation. For example, a parent warns a child not to touch an electrical socket because if he does, he will get electrocuted. Of course, that wouldn't happen from touching a socket. It seems to me it is human nature to embellish when someone's safety is at stake.

"That a girl," Satan said as Eve took a bite of the fruit and gave the rest to Adam. "See?" he chided. "Nothing happened."

Eve looked embarrassed, and I could tell she wondered if Adam could be trusted to hear from God. Their relationship had already changed. She would have never have thought such a thing before the fruit.

The show was over as far as the other demons were concerned. They turned and headed back to Satan's den, slapping one another on the back and celebrating how easy it was for Satan to get Earth back. I knew things weren't over yet, so I stayed around to see what would happen when God showed up, as He was sure to do.

I climbed up on my perch and tried to figure out what the real problem was with what Adam and Eve had done. To be candid, I expected God might think it over and give them a pass. A rational mind would have to conclude this episode did not merit changing the destiny of Earth. Adam and Eve wanted to know the difference between good and evil. So who doesn't? Later on I would hear God tell people a thousand times to flee from evil. How does one flee from evil if he doesn't know what evil looks like?

They wanted to be like God; again, who doesn't? As time passed, I would hear humans sing about wanting to be more like God, with God liking every note of it. Why is it fine for future generations to want to be like God, but not them?

Was any of what Satan said to them true? Not really. Their eyes were opened to things they hadn't paid attention to before, but those things had always been there. The first thing they saw was their nakedness. They had never been anything but naked. They just hadn't noticed. I don't know how they saw themselves prior to this, but being naked was apparently a big surprise to them. They sewed fig leaves together and made coverings for themselves. With this new knowledge Satan had promised them, they somehow connected being naked with knowing good and evil. Who knows?

When they heard the rustling of the trees and felt the coolness of the air, they both took off in different directions and nose-dived into the underbrush. God had arrived.

God called, "Adam, where are you?"

Adam crouched down and did not say a word. I knew how he felt as he hid behind a palm tree, hoping God would not find him. I found myself remembering the sorrow, fear, and self-loathing that overwhelmed me when I realized that by my own ambivalence, I had disobeyed God and separated myself from Him forever. Why did I listen to Lucifer?

As I heard God call for Adam again, I began to feel sad, hurt, and angry about it. God was actually seeking after this disobedient creature. God had never searched or called out to me after the rebellion. I hadn't really done anything wrong, not like Adam anyway. Adam knew the rule and intentionally disobeyed. I was a victim of circumstances. If God had cared the slightest thing about me, He should have realized it and given me a second chance.

At God's third call, Adam sheepishly stepped from behind the tree. He looked like a tree himself, decked out in his new leaf clothing.

"Adam," God said, "why didn't you come when I called?"

Adam didn't work very hard on his answer. "I heard You in the garden, and I was afraid because I was naked, so I hid."

Then God replied, "Who said you were naked? Did you eat from the forbidden tree?"

Adam looked around for Eve and, not seeing her, leaned in and whispered to God, "Yes, but it wasn't my fault. The woman You put here with me made me do it. She gave me some fruit from the tree and insisted I eat it."

Satan blew his cover as a snake when he roared with delight as he heard what Adam said.

Right then Eve stepped out into the clearing and stood behind Adam. Unaware she was there, Adam continued to explain to God how this was Eve's fault. I could see her face clearly as she listened to Adam accuse her. I'm quite sure that if I had been capable of pity, I would have had it for Eve that day. She was crushed and horrified. She could barely assimilate the idea that this man upon whom she had depended, believed, and loved was now willing to sacrifice her to the certain wrath of God.

An awful thing happened in that moment for humanity. A breach occurred between men and women that has never been successfully mended. Satan would nest forever in that breach. Both of them were truly horrified when they realized that their enticer ridiculed them in the presence of God.

"Kill them," Satan ranted to God. "They defied You like I told You they would. Destroy them for their ambition. Just like You did it to me, now do it to them."

God's eyes blazed as He turned from Adam and Eve and faced Satan, who stopped ranting and fell down under the weight of His gaze, laying still on the ground in front of Him.

When I saw the wrath in God's eyes, I was too terrified to continue watching. I tucked my head under my wing and pretended I hadn't seen a thing.

CHAPTER 13

I TRIED HUMMING A tune so I would not hear what God said to the serpent. "Hmm..."

Humming is not a natural skill for angels, and I had a little trouble getting a rhythm for it. Finally I ran out of breath and gave up. I did not want to hear because I had no desire to be the only witness to Satan's further humiliation. When I couldn't hum any longer, I couldn't help myself. I heard every word.

God told the serpent, "Because you've done this, you're cursed beyond all cattle and wild animals, cursed to slink on your belly and eat dirt all your life."

It was amazing to see. The serpent began a meltdown before them. His legs and arms contracted, and he turned into the serpent you humans are familiar with: long, full of scales, and when he tried to speak, he could only hiss.

His teeth became fangs filled with poison—a bad idea if you ask me. The serpent wriggled violently, and I knew it was Satan trying to escape the serpent's body, but God would not let him go. He held him captive inside the snake until He finished speaking.

OK, I know I said earlier that Satan shape-shifted. It made sense at the moment, but hearing the curse made me rethink things. Maybe it was not shape-shifting I saw, but a kind of possession.

Until God spoke the curse, it had not occurred to me whether the serpent might have been complicit in some way with Satan's scheme. Otherwise, why curse a helpless animal? Before Satan seduced Adam and Eve, my guess is he first charmed the serpent to allow him to use his body.

Shape-shifting or animal possession—it doesn't really matter. The deed had been done. I thought about asking Satan about it but gave up the idea. The answer would not be worth the beating.

God continued, "I'm declaring war between you and the woman, between your offspring and hers. He'll crush your head, and you'll wound his heel."

I had already figured out that offspring had something to do with that multiply and subdue commandment from earlier. But what could God have possibly meant when He said Satan was going to have offspring? How was that going to happen? Not wanting to miss a word, I hung as far over the ledge as I dared without falling off.

I couldn't believe Satan didn't jump on that idea right away. He didn't seem one bit mystified or interested in the offspring comment as it pertained to him. God released Satan from the serpent that slithered away very quickly. Satan pulled himself together as best he could and more or less slumped over. Unable to stand upright before God, Satan must have been truly terrified, thinking this time He would certainly destroy him completely. Otherwise, I'm sure he would have insisted on more clarity on the bizarre notion of offspring.

God surprised me when He allowed Satan to escape the garden unscathed. One might have thought the enemy of both man and God would be feeling victorious after his bloodless coup, stealing Earth from Adam and Eve. Instead, when he summoned me to his den, he seemed nervous. He demanded I recount all that happened in the garden encounter with God. I was afraid when I realized he knew I had listened to the whole thing.

I tried to explain. "I wasn't paying that much attention. I barely heard anything."

"Liar," he shouted at me rising from his seat. I assumed the groveling position and he sat back down.

"Tell me exactly what He said. Don't change any of the words," he demanded.

I raised my head a little. "I wasn't eavesdropping, sir," I wanted to be sure he didn't think I was spying on him.

"Don't grovel, imbecile."

"Right, I just thought I should explain why I happened to overhear..."

He cut me off. "Do not think. Watch and report, nothing more."

"Yes, of course, not a problem," I quickly agreed. Then I sat very still waiting for his reply.

"Then tell me what He said, you idiot!" Clenching his claws and grinding his teeth, he shouted at me loud enough for all creation to hear. I was terribly embarrassed by it, but that did not quell his rudeness the slightest little bit. He continued, "How long must I endure your ineptitude? Just tell me what you heard Him say."

"Right, well, it was something like this," I began. "Cursed is the ground—"

He interrupted. "Not that part, after that."

"Right," I jumped ahead, "and cursed are you above the livestock—"

"After that," he interrupted again.

"You will crawl on your belly—" before I could finish the sentence, he threw a stone right at me.

"After that, toward the end," he dropped his head to rest on his claw and waved me on with the other one.

"Oh, right, I know what part you mean." Obviously, God's comment about offspring had not gone right by him after all.

"God said He was declaring war between your offspring and the offspring of the woman." I stopped right there, thinking that was the intriguing part. But, he waved me to go still further.

"The last line, give me the last line." He sighed as if weary of the whole ordeal.

"God said something about you striking the heel of her offspring and then her offspring would stomp on your head and crush it to dust." He glared at me.

"God said He would stomp on my head?" he demanded.

"More or less," I realized I shouldn't have added my own translation. His eyes shot fire at me. I tried to amend what I said. "Actually, now as I recall, maybe it wasn't quite that." He glared at me more fiercely, and I backed up more trying not to trip over my tail.

"Now I remember," I managed to get the words out. "It was more like her offspring will crush your head, but I'm sure He did not mean it literally."

Satan drew back and sat down on his throne, saying nothing more. I didn't know what to do, so I stood there. He went deep into his own thoughts, and when I was sure he was no longer aware of whether I was in the room or not, I crept out as quickly and quietly as possible.

I went back to my perch to see if anyone was still in the garden. I wondered if God had destroyed Adam or Eve or both of them for their disobedience. Instead, I saw God was talking to the woman. Adam stood by; both of them looked ashamed about the whole thing, but he said nothing. I strained to listen to God's soft voice and then could not believe what I was hearing.

"Eve," God said in the most tender tone. "You sinned against Me. Why?"

"The serpent beguiled me, and I believed him," Eve whispered, her eyes full of sorrow at what she had done.

Then God turned to Adam. "Adam, you sinned against Me, knowing full well what you were doing. Then you hid from Me and blamed Eve for your actions." God's voice was quiet but stern.

Adam shuffled his feet in the leaves and shifted his weight uncomfortably, but he did not reply.

God continued to speak to the man. "Your intentional, unrepentant sin prevents you from remaining in Eden. I told you to obey Me in just one thing. Was that too much to ask? " I could tell God was grieved by the judgment He was about to pronounce on Adam. "You must leave. You cannot stay in Eden."

Then God turned back to Eve. "Eve, because you were deceived, your sin is not as onerous to me as that of Adam. Do you want to stay in the garden without Adam?"

"What did He say?" I blurted out to no one at all as I tripped over myself, trying to get to the edge of second heaven to hear better. I could not be hearing God correctly.

God continued, "You may stay here, and I will watch over you, or you may go into exile with your husband."

Eve looked over to Adam, who pleaded with her with his eyes not to abandon him, although, in my mind, he had been perfectly willing to do that to her. God saw the pain and sympathy in Eve's eyes as she looked back at Adam.

"If you go with him," God spoke softly, "then your desire will be to please him. He will misinterpret your love for weakness and he will rule over you."

Adam did not dare say a word, but his eyes said it all. "I won't, I promise. I'll take care of you. I'll love you." It was all right there in the tears welling up and spilling over his cheeks. Eve was distressed as she looked first to God then to Adam.

I could not stand it anymore. I leaned over the edge and shouted at Eve, not caring who in heaven or Earth might hear me.

"Eve! Listen to me. Don't do it. Adam is not worth it. Stay in the garden with God. Nothing is worth being separated from Him."

When I heard her say she would go with Adam, I collapsed in a heap of emotional exhaustion. I did not have the energy to climb back on my perch. I sprawled there on the rim with one claw and half my tail hanging precariously over the edge of the abyss. I didn't know whether God was as distressed with her choice as I was, but if He was, He did nothing to show it. I thought He would leave them right then, but He didn't. In fact, He did something completely unexpected, and, dare I say, out of character. He made garments of skin for Adam and Eve.

"Why does He think they need more clothing?" I muttered. "If He thinks they need apparel, why not let them keep the coverings of leaves?"

That would have made much more sense since the garden was quite warm and much better suited to grass skirts than wool and fur. They were going to be conspicuously overdressed for their surroundings.

That by itself was not the "out-of-character" part I mentioned earlier. In order to make clothes of skins for them, God had to kill one of His wonderful animals and shed its blood. Now think about that for a moment. To God, the giver of life, all life is precious. He did not destroy the rebellious angels, some of whom most certainly needed to be destroyed; yet here He was sacrificing the life of an innocent animal.

"For what?" I asked myself, "So Adam and Eve could have more useless clothes, which they did not need to start with?"

I have pondered this question for a very long time, and until now I haven't figured it out. It had to have something to do with the blood, but what?

So the Lord God exiled Adam and Eve from the Garden of Eden to work and sweat over the ground from which they had been made. After He drove them out, He placed cherubim on the east side of the garden where they stood vigilant with their flaming swords flashing back and forth to guard the way to the tree of life.

Having chosen the tree of the knowledge of good and evil, Adam and Eve were banished from their home and never allowed to return.

I knew just how they felt.

CHAPTER 14

THE MORE I thought about Adam and Eve's meltdown in the garden, the more I found myself annoyed with God about how He handled it. They committed intentional sin, and yet their entire punishment consisted of being moved outside the garden to another perfectly acceptable place on the planet. Furthermore, contrary to what I thought would happen and what *should have* happened, God continued to watch over them. I sinned against God by accident, and look what happened to me—thrown out of paradise to a foreign place with no chance to appeal my sentence.

Why should humans and nobody else get a pass—or at least a second chance—when it comes to sin? I've now chronicled humanity through several generations of Adam and Eve's kids, and I can tell you there has not been any noticeable improvement in any of them. For someone with the responsibility for worlds and universes beyond the scope of earthly imagination, God was spending way too much time trying to fix humans. He does so until this day. Why does He keep trying to make you people into something you cannot be? He gives you much more credit for using your intelligence than you deserve. Mankind falls into such a predictable pattern of behavior, it isn't entertaining to watch anymore.

Act one: God gives people a choice between obedience and rebellion. Act two: they always rebel. Act three: He finds a loophole in the law and forgives them. End of play. Then the cycle starts again. Humanity does not learn a thing from experience. That's why I cannot understand why He didn't save Himself millennia of grief by canceling the mandate to Adam and Eve to multiply.

"Cut your losses," I would have told Him. "Start with a fresh batch of clay and forget the free will thing altogether."

Surely He must have known that any offspring born of Adam and Eve would be just like them. And indeed that is what happened.

God was right when He warned Eve that her childbearing would come through great pain. Cain came screaming from Eve, who was in writhing pain and all alone because Adam had passed out at the first glimpse of Cain's bloody head emerging. I don't know how Adam thought he was going to get any kids, but I'm confident this was nowhere in his thinking. One can hardly blame him, though. His only experience with new life was when he took a nap, woke up, and there was Eve—all cleaned up and pretty, fully functional and able to take care of herself from day one. He probably thought it was always going to be like that.

Eve was mostly on her own in birthing the baby. It made me nervous to watch. In my mind, no other human experience would more clearly define the difference between man and woman than childbirth. Man will endure pain for what is to be gained by it. Woman will endure pain for what is to be loved, with no guarantee that she will be loved in return.

Eve loved her children so intently before they were born that she endured her own body splitting apart to give them life. Adam liked the kids once he got used to them, but I can tell you that if it had been up to him to give birth, the entire human population would have stopped at three. In fact, when Eve told him she was going to have another baby, Adam told her to figure out what was causing it and quit doing it.

Although Adam and Eve would live the rest of their lives with the consequences of their sin, God was still incredibly kind to them. They knew He was helping them, though He never dropped by for a walk anymore. They wanted their children to know about Him, so they were forever telling stories about God and how He continued to take care of them and teach them. My opinion is they were trying to find ways to make up for what they had done in the garden. As a matter of fact, the whole idea of humans offering something back to God from their earthly labor started with the two of them. I thought it was silly. God is in need of nothing that His creation could offer Him. Surely they must have known that.

Yet, they were sacrificing food or whatever to Him as if they thought He must have to eat like they did. You can imagine my surprise when I realized God Himself was the One who gave them the idea to do it.

If true justice prevailed, they were supposed to be living under a curse and deprived of any special consideration from God. Now, I ask you, how would a reasonable person understand a curse? A curse, in my mind, means no supernatural intervention—none at all. That's what I got; no sympathy whatsoever. Throw them out and let them make it on their own, I say.

But here was God coming up with a scheme by which He could get around His own rules and give them whatever they needed. By giving some of the fruit of their labor back to the Lord, He now had a legal method to bless their work and their obedience. I no longer had any compassion for them at all. They taught their children to do the same in returning part of their earnings to God. Before long, I could see how offering God the first portion of something He didn't need to start with was a form of interaction, communion you might say, with God. So much for living under a curse.

Cain, the first son, went into agriculture. He thought the offering ritual was silly and that God couldn't possibly need the crop as badly as he did. Cain went along with it because it was easier to do it than argue all day long with his parents about it. Nonetheless, Cain was always looking for a way to minimize his losses. When it was time for the offering, Cain would present God with a plant that looked like it was going to die anyway. Then he would make a big show out of offering it up. The Lord, as I knew would be the case, was unimpressed, so much so that He blew the smoke of the offering right back in Cain's face.

Abel, the second boy, got the hang of giving first-fruits right away. He made his living tending the flocks because he was good with animals. He never seemed to begrudge the offering ritual in the least. It seemed he rather looked forward to it. He would take the best part of the animal, dedicate it to God, and then burn it up right there before Him on an altar. Then Abel would take the rest for himself.

Until this happened, Satan had not paid that much attention to Adam and Eve's kids. But when he heard the rest of us talking about the petulant Cain, he sparked to immediate attention. He walked to the edge of second heaven and watched intently to see if there would be a further exchange between Cain and God. And, of course, you know there was.

God let Cain stew in his pity for a while and then spoke to him. "Why are you angry, Cain? What's the matter with you?"

Cain did not answer. He put his hands in his pockets and kicked some leaves around with his foot.

"You must do what is right," God went on. "If you persist in offense, sin will overtake you. Cain, start now. You must master it." God almost pleaded with him

The dawn of understanding cracked open for me when I heard that. A lot of things I had been unable to comprehend suddenly became clear. I should have seen it before. Satan is going to need human beings if he wants to get anything done on Earth. If God restricted Himself to work through mankind, Satan would have to do the same.

Satan hurried back to his lair and summoned one of the most loathsome of our kind to his private chambers. His name was Murder. Satan assigned Murder to go down to Earth and shadow Cain. When Cain thought about how God had embarrassed him, Murder was to affirm his feelings by entering into the conversation Cain was having with himself. Ever so seductively, Murder crept into Cain's mind.

Murder reminded Cain of every childhood incident where Abel was favored. He would tell him Abel plotted to make Cain's offering look meager.

"Why would Abel offer such an extravagant sacrifice if not to shame your efforts?" Murder whispered.

As Cain's offense grew against Abel, Murder was to watch for the moment when Cain's self-pity swallowed up his common sense so that he blamed God for His unfairness. When it happened, and it did, Murder sailed through the open door into Cain's soul.

One might think Cain would have lost his ability to make choices after more or less becoming a slave to Murder's orders. Not so. Cain's spirit warred against the intrusion of Murder into his soul. Two out of three wins, so it would be Cain's flesh that would choose between the desires of the soul and the demands of the spirit. The design flaw in humanity's makeup could never have been more evident than at that moment.

I make no pretense to be smarter than God, but even I would have known not to use flesh and blood as building materials in creating a reasoning life form. Flesh is fickle, inferior, and completely unreliable in a crisis. Its demands are never satisfied, and it's in need of constant maintenance. It is easily enticed, manipulated, and bargains for very little. The souls of men would not have near the casualties if it were not for their skin, blood, and bones.

Things might have turned out quite differently if it had not been for Cain's soulish desires. I feel certain his mind would have overcome his emotions had it not been for the pleasure of revenge, which caused his skin to tingle in anticipation. Cain was probably still thinking it over when he asked Abel to go for a walk with him.

Cain found his brother with the cows. "Let's go out to the field."

Abel tried to engage him in friendly chitchat, but Cain was not much of a conversationalist that day. His mind was consumed with listening to Murder speak into his inner ear.

"Do you want to know why your brother deliberately made you look foolish in front of your parents?" Murder whispered.

Cain was listening, and as he did so, Murder slipped deeper into Cain's consciousness and unleashed a power into Cain that exhilarated him beyond anything he had ever felt.

Murder continued, "It's about the inheritance. You're out of the will now. When they die they will leave everything to Abel. He will drive you away."

"I'll be destitute to wander Earth with no place to live," Cain said in his own mind.

Murder didn't have to say another word. Cain's mind took over at that point, and as the demonic power surged within him, he talked himself into fratricide.

"Abel has tried to turn my parents against me all my life. He won't get away with it," Cain assured himself.

Ecstatic with the demon's power coursing through his soul, and lusting for revenge, Cain picked up a stone and attacked his brother and killed him.

For less than an instant, Cain was thrilled by his power over life. The adrenaline surge satisfied his need for revenge. But he had only a moment to revel in his sense of invincibility; as quickly as Murder had seized Cain, he left, taking his power with him. Cain fought to retain the ecstasy that bled out of his soul, but he could not. He slumped over, weak, mortified, and full of fear.

Murder couldn't fly fast enough to get back to Satan's lair to brag about his success.

"Just like his old man," Murder laughed, "dumber than dirt." Satan roared and slapped Murder on the back with his claw in that silly way we males have of congratulating each other.

Cain looked at his slain brother on the ground before him and became horribly afraid.

"What have I done?" He dropped to his knees and tried to revive his slain brother. Cain lifted the bleeding head of Abel and tried to remember why he had hated him so. He dropped Abel's head and jumped to his feet as if trying to grasp something that was no longer there. Where was the awesome power that he felt moments before? Where had it gone, and why was he now in such deep despair?

Satan roared with satisfaction at the whimpering Cain who had been so easily seduced by Murder. In fear of being discovered, Cain dug a shallow grave and buried Abel. Then he ran as far as he could until the weight of God's presence bore down upon him, driving him to his knees.

God said, "Where is your brother Abel?"

"I don't know," he replied. "Am I my brother's keeper?"

I wanted to shout out, "Bad answer, Cain," but, of course, I did not for fear of being overheard by you-know-who. Oh, but if I could have advised him, I knew I could have gotten him a lighter sentence. I've watched God and humans long enough to know God's soft spot.

"Cain," I would have said. "Lose the machismo. Repent. Beg for forgiveness. Grovel. I know God. He loves that stuff. Trust me, it will work." But, of course, I said nothing.

God said, "What have you done? Your brother's blood cries to Me from the ground where you buried him. You've brought a curse on the land. From now on you'll get nothing but failed crops. This won't be your home any longer, and you'll be a restless wanderer on Earth."

Cain got the very thing he so feared—the curse he had only a day before pronounced upon himself. Still on his knees, Cain whimpered to God, "This is not fair. This punishment is more than I can stand."

I was disgusted with the whole charade. "Cain," I shouted, no longer caring who heard me, "can you be more of a wimp? Banished from your land? You call that punishment? Let me tell you about punishment. How about if God expelled you from the planet? How about being left alone to float endlessly in space? You are still alive and on the same earth where you were born, and yet you whine like a sniveling coward?"

When I thought he could not get any more pathetic, he whined some more.

Cain said to God, "My punishment is too much. I can't take it! You've thrown me off the land, and I can never again face You. I'm a homeless wanderer on Earth, and whoever finds me will kill me."

Then God said to him, "Not so. If anyone kills you, he will suffer vengeance seven times over." Then God put a mark on Cain's head so that no one who found him would harm him. God went home, and Cain went on to live happily ever after in the land of Nod, east of Eden.

I simply could not believe it had happened again; another pass for humanity. I wanted to fly after God and demand a hearing. "God, if you are going to punish those who sin against You, at least be consistent. Where do You get off letting a murderer go free? Is that what You call punishment? Why does he get another chance? Why didn't I?"

I slouched back to my perch, covered my head with my wings, and groused at the unfairness of it all.

Cain got married and had many children. Adam and Eve conceived again, and Seth was born. He too married and had many children, and the whole population of Earth grew. While this went on for decades, Satan remained somewhat passive as far as humans were concerned. Ages came and went, and while the demons were allowed to vex the humans from time to time, Satan seemed oddly disengaged with the whole thing.

Then one day, he turned his attention to the ruling principalities over Earth. They had been in place since Earth was created and were the very powerful angels who had authority to govern the affairs of Earth before Satan stole it. The fact they remained at their posts and the fact that Satan thought he needed an army meant there was sure to be a fight at some point. I stayed away from them myself, not knowing where their loyalties might be in light of the Fall, humans, and all that.

When I saw Satan flying toward them, I knew he had a plan. Another kind of war was about to be unleashed upon Earth.

CHAPTER 15

I COULD NEVER HAVE been a member of the elite
angel league, of course, but many others were
chosen, hundreds of them. God had a lot of ideas
about the countries and continents mankind would
discover on Earth, but He also knew humanity would
have no idea where to start. To help humans get the
hang of managing the many challenges in bringing order
and stability to their growing society, God appointed
protectors from the mightiest of the angelic guard and
set them in government over each of the divisions of the
planet. As it always was with Him, when He gave power
and authority, it was an irrevocable gift.

By now, can you figure out what a wretchedly bad
idea that was? How could anyone who hoped to main-
tain peace and devotion to oneself ever suppose that the
combination of irreversible power, authority, supernatural

ability, and free will might be a good idea? Someone on the council should have warned God about what could happen in a setup like that.

That is how it came to be that these mighty ones were established in provincial reign over Earth, helping humanity learn to manage the planet. But before these angels were assigned to Earth, they were in third heaven. Like all the angels, they were under the authority of the archangels, the chief among them being Lucifer.

Because most of them had been trained under Lucifer before he went bad and became Satan, they recognized him immediately when he approached, in spite of the fact that he now looked like the last three days of a misspent life. The mighty ones had not followed him into rebellion, but their prior familiarity with him and the natural curiosity that we angels have left open an unfortunate door that God should have thought about and closed off at once.

I would never have had the nerve to do it, but Satan was not even a trifle reluctant about approaching the awesome angelic brigade. Knowing how sly and disarming he can be, I would have expected them to have their guard up when they saw him coming. Perhaps they thought there was little to fear from this battle-scarred old archangel. Or maybe they were simply curious and wanted to hear Satan's side of the story for themselves. More likely they had forgotten how cunning and crafty he really is.

Every one of the demons in second heaven gathered on the ledge and tittered nervously among themselves like schoolgirls at a sock hop as they watched Satan approach the prince of Persia. I was apprehensive, but I stood by as well and hoped they wouldn't come after us.

"Hail, mighty one, son of God," Satan called out to the prince as he bowed low before the surprised angel.

Although he tried to appear nonchalant about it, one could not miss the twinkle in the prince's eyes that betrayed his pride at receiving such a greeting from his former superior. I wished I could have been a voice of reason in the prince's ear. I would have warned him of what was sure to happen.

"You do not know what Lucifer has become," I would have whispered. "He isn't here to chat with you. Run! Run like the wind. If he is talking, he is lying. He will flatter you, and you will believe him, and then you will want to hear more."

The mighty prince of Persia puffed up like a toasted marshmallow as Satan lavished him with praise. No doubt he would have drawn his sword and lopped Satan's claw off if he had only known how many times his former mentor had derided him before God. When Lucifer, as he was known then, learned of his judgment, he slandered all of the other heavenly beings, especially the mighty ones who ruled Earth. Now here he was, fairly groveling as he bowed down before the prince and flattered him with all sorts of unbelievable adulation. By the time Satan set the trap, this "mighty" one stepped right in.

Satan did what he does best. He asked a question, "Have you considered the daughters of men?"

For a moment, I was paralyzed by the horror at what I knew was coming next. Someone must stop him. I tapped and tugged at the leering demons there on the ledge, trying to get someone to listen to me.

"Stop him! Stop him before it's too late," I pleaded.

They rebuffed me and pushed me away from where they stood.

"He knows what he's doing," one said.

"We don't need your opinion," another added, "Get to the back of the line and leave us alone."

"No, you must listen to me," I begged as I tried to wiggle my way in among them again. "God will not stand for it. I know what I'm talking about. You must listen to me."

But they would not. They kept watching and sneering with delight at the transaction under way between Satan and the prince. I had to try again.

"Don't you see what is happening?" I screamed at their lustful faces. "If he succeeds in tempting the mighty ones to breach the forbidden zone, it will be the end of us all. God will not hold back. He will not show mercy."

"Mercy?" the ugly one snarled. "What mercy did we ever receive? We were banished, thrown out, discarded as if we had never mattered."

I shot back, "You are still alive, you fool. God let you live. He let us live instead of turning us to ash, as He could have. If Satan does this thing, we will be cast forevermore to Tartaroo."

He drew back for a moment at my words. We knew about Tartaroo, the deepest part of hell reserved for rebellious angels.

"Then we will reign there," he bragged.

"Is there no limit to your stupidity? For once in your pitiful existence, just try to think five minutes ahead. Are you so thick-skulled that eternal damnation means nothing to you?"

Demons do not respond well to constructive criticism.

When I regained consciousness, I tried desperately to remember what happened to cause me to be hanging upside down by my tail over the jagged edge of the cliff that rimmed second heaven. I was bewildered and completely helpless, dangling over the abyss below. One of my wings was broken, and my eyes were swollen shut. I could feel several loose teeth. When I opened my mouth to moan in pain, one actually fell out and tumbled into the blackness below. Everything about me hurt: my hooves, my claws, my scales, and my other wing had a tear in it.

It was awhile before I could recollect what I had done to get myself into such a fix. I hung there in the darkness for the longest time, trying to get my fragmented memory back together. When the image of Satan and the prince came crashing back into my consciousness, I was terrified. I had to get down. I swung myself back and forth in hopes that my tail would break off and I would at last fall into the bottomless darkness below me. Whatever was down there would not be as bad as the wrath I knew would soon be loosed from third heaven.

"Perhaps the abyss won't be that bad," I said to my quaking self. "Perhaps I will fall forever and simply cease to exist."

I swung harder, but my tail did not break off; it only hurt more.

"Limbo," I muttered, "I'm caught in limbo. I can't go down and I can't get up. Help! Help! Help!" I shouted to a demonic horde that was no longer there and would not have responded even if they had been.

I should have known no one was going to help me the least little bit. I flapped my working wing for all it was worth until I was able to levitate upward to the edge of the cliff. I grabbed hold with my good claw and pulled myself up until I could rest my cracked head and broken appendage on the ledge. I unwound my tail from the protruded stone below where I had hung for who knows how long. Somehow I was able to pull the rest of me up until I lay on the rim, exhausted and wishing I were dead. After a while, I crawled back to my perch and waited to see what would happen next.

I felt the sound before I heard it. I cringed into a ball at the blood-curdling screams coming from the women of Earth. For all the horror we had wrought upon Earth, there had never been a sound of despair like this. The floor of second heaven reverberated as the cries from the women went up and up and up until it was only a matter of moments until they would pierce through this realm and reach third heaven. Soon God would respond to the terrible thing that had happened on Earth.

The sanctity of mankind had been breached. The mighty ones, incited to indulge their lust by the deceitfulness of Satan, transgressed their own nature to violate the daughters of men. The holy angels surrendered to sexual immorality and went after the forbidden flesh of human women, condemning themselves to suffer His vengeance in eternal fire.

Satan danced and laughed from the safety of second heaven as Earth reeled at the rape of the women. Freaks and giants would soon be born, and many mothers would die in agony in their birthing. In their lust, some of the mighty ones went after the human men and the men became insane from the violation and in turn deposited their seed into the animals. The gene pool of all human and animal life was degraded beyond redemption.

"How do you like it now, God?" Satan jeered toward heaven.

And for a moment, it seemed as if Satan had finally won, his revenge accomplished against the mighty angelic guard, who had remained faithful to God in the cosmic rebellion and now plunged into the unquenchable fire of His wrath for degrading His most prized creation.

"Woe to Earth," I moaned. A species God did not create was now in the midst of mankind.

The Nephilim were upon the earth.

CHAPTER 16

I T WAS HORRIBLE. They were awful. A half-breed demon turned out to be far worse than a demon in its natural state, and much more dangerous. A regular garden-variety demon, as all of us were, had limitations when it came to our ability to interact with humans. We who were part of the fall could create circumstances that would cause humans to do terrible things to each other, but we ourselves could not actually touch any of them. God left a gaping hole in security when He failed to anticipate that the faithful angels might at some point rebel, because He neglected to place the same prohibition on them.

I suppose it never crossed God's mind that His elite force might think to be anything but helpful to mankind. They would never have dared be any other way to this new life form God seemed to favor so much. That is surely the reason God's wrath was unleashed upon them so ferociously. They weren't condemned to a fallen state in second heaven as we were. Much worse, they were judged right there on the spot and thrown down to the dreaded Tartaroo. Let me tell you, our punishment had been but a swat on the backside compared to their complete banishment.

It seemed that Satan had won in that regard as well. The faithful elite guard who failed to follow him in the cosmic rebellion ended up being caught in yet another of his webs of deception. Satan's revenge on the heavenly host was now satisfied.

I don't know why, but it was unsettling to me that God had not anticipated something like the Nephilim. As a result, they carried a human gene, and it gave them legal access to afflict humans directly. No seduction, clever ruses, or half-truths were necessary. If a Nephilim wanted to devour a human, it just took one.

Satan wanted to throw a party to celebrate his triumph over heaven and Earth, so he released upon the Nephilim all of the spirits of lust he had held in captivity. They went wild. The demons in second heaven danced around, vicariously participating in the revelry and gloating as if they held some great victory in their hands. I really wanted to join in. It gets tiresome being the only one who sees the cloud behind every silver lining. I couldn't get in the mood when I knew the celebrating was premature. How could they have forgotten what God was like?

Maybe I should have tried to warn them again.

"Better yet," I said to myself, "maybe not."

After all, I was still feeling the beating I had endured at their claws when I tried to reason with them before, only to be left hanging upside down over the abyss for my trouble. My equilibrium had not righted itself either, and I was fearful of tipping over and giving them something else to ridicule. I picked up my injured tail and slunk off to find a place to lie down.

"Fools," I was tempted to shout at the reveling demons. "Don't you know God is brooding over Earth this very minute? No matter how it looks at the moment, this is not going to end well."

Instead, I said nothing. It wasn't worth another pounding from them just to be proven right later on.

"We've won! We've won!" they shouted in their drunken delight as the lustful Nephilim ravaged every living thing upon Earth.

And I have to admit, the longer it went on, the more it looked as if they might be right. After all, God imposed upon Himself the rules of engagement over Earth. If mankind could not redeem it, then Earth would be Satan's possession forever. Not only had Adam and Eve failed miserably, but now the whole gene pool of man and beast was corrupted beyond redemption. God would have to scrap it and start over with a new batch if He wanted to continue trying to make the humanity thing work. There was no way I could see for God to get around having to destroy the whole Earth and everything in it. Satan saw it as well. He was delirious with anticipation.

The whole demonic horde was irrepressible in their glee at the seeming certainty of having Earth back to do as they pleased. Since God had restored it so marvelously from the devastation of Lucifer's flood (in preparation for Adam, of course), it was in great shape. All of them were excited to have it back to rule over again without interference.

As the mayhem continued and God seemed to be doing nothing but stalling for time, I started to feel a little less nervous about a terrible retribution. God simply could not fix this and stay within the rules, so I wondered if He had decided to accept the inevitable—Earth was lost to Him.

Although things looked bad for God, somehow I knew it wasn't over. That's why I continued to watch Earth, just in case. I wanted to go inside to get away from the tremors, which were making me queasy. It had been happening for days now. The atmosphere shuddered under the weight of God's eyes as He searched to and fro about Earth. He was looking for something I suppose, but for what, I could not guess.

After a while, it looked like it might finally be over. I was about to give it up and go party with the others when company came. I should say came and went. He rocketed past me faster than a lightning bolt, singed my injured wing, and knocked me over as He passed through second heaven without slowing down. Nothing was left in His wake but the clashing of thunder as the air He had split crashed back together. Oh, I knew who it was all right. It was Him—Ruah Ha Kadosh—racing to Earth below.

"Why is He going down there this late in the game?" I wondered. I moved back to the edge and followed the trail of light that flowed after Him, enabling me to track His movements. Tracking Him may be a bit of an over-statement since I could not actually see where He was but only where He had been.

I was about to be proven right again. When I was sure of what He was doing down there, I left my post and went inside with the revelers to give Satan the news. I tried sauntering into the party room as I had seen Satan do when he wanted to pretend that he wasn't really worried. Sauntering was apparently not in my skill set. The partying stopped short and every eye darted my way as if I had walked into the room with an off switch that abruptly stopped the festivities.

Satan saw my expression and glared at me as if daring me to bring bad news. "You saw something. What was it?" he growled.

"They missed one, sir," I stammered. "The Nephilim—they missed one."

"One what?" Satan demanded.

"A human being, your majesty; they missed him, one uncorrupted man. He must have gotten away during the raids," I explained.

Satan spun rapidly and pointed his claw at one of the largest demons.

"Get down there! Find out who it is." Satan yelled as if the demon were off in another dimension instead of five feet away.

"No, wait," I blurted out before my mind caught up with my mouth. "It's too late."

"Too late?" Satan snarled, daring me to tell him something he did not want to hear.

"Ruah Ha Kadosh—He's already there. He found a man named Noah."

I tucked my tail and hunkered down just in case, but to my surprise, Satan did not swing at me as he usually did when he had nothing else to do with his frustration. The look in his eyes was not so much anger as shock. He didn't say or do anything at all right then. He dropped his noisemaker by his side; the party was over. He walked out to my perch, climbed up on it, and looked down at Earth. He sat there for a long time and then began to mumble to himself.

"The Nephilim are hunters; how did they miss him? Where was he hiding?" As he walked back toward his den, he snapped at me. "Listen to every word. Let nothing happen that I don't hear about before it happens."

So I hopped back on my perch, and I listened.

This is where it gets hard to explain what I saw. Ruah Ha Kadosh was clearly talking to Noah; I heard Him. But because no one can really *see* where He is at any given moment, only where He's been, it looked like Noah was talking to the thin air.

"Noah, you are a righteous man and have found favor with God," the voice said.

Noah was a righteous man. That's what I heard Him say.

But what exactly did He mean by "righteous"? Satan would want to know. Certainly neither Noah nor his family had copulated with the mighty ones, but to be honest about it, he was not the only one on Earth who could say that. Maybe Noah had not broken any of God's rules.

"No," I reasoned. "That cannot be it. God hasn't made any more rules since that incident with the trees in Eden." Mankind had only one rule to obey, and look what happened. God was not about to make things worse by giving him any more. Whatever it was that had made Noah righteous, it was not about *not* doing something God had forbidden.

I looked over my left wing to see if the party had resumed, but it hadn't. It was eerily quiet. The other demons had gone back to their common lair. I had a clear line of sight to Satan's throne, where he sat staring at nothing.

He had not anticipated Noah. Now he had to regroup.

CHAPTER 17

M Y ASSIGNMENT WAS to stay on guard and watch how things developed with Noah. Satan wanted to know if God's declaration about him being righteous might have a loophole in it somewhere.

"I hope so," I thought. "Maybe I can improve my standing with the group if I can report how I've found a legal technicality that might void the whole deal."

God continued to talk to Noah. "I am going to put an end to all people because Earth has become a sewer filled with violence and degradation. I am surely going to destroy every living thing. So make yourself an ark of cypress wood with rooms in it, and coat it with pitch inside and out."

Noah did not answer God. But if he had, by the look on his face, the whole of his reply would have been, "OK, whatever." Noah did not come close to grasping the enormity of what God had said. God announced an extinction-level event, yet Noah failed to emit the slightest gasp. I wondered if God was a little disappointed in Noah's lack of enthusiasm.

I have a theory about how God wired humans. It's like He put a genetic code in their central nervous system to link them with their ancestors and descendants through a corporate memory, so to speak. The code and memory somehow keep them linked to one another across the centuries. That's why it's not uncommon for a person to look like or behave like a distant relative who lived long before. No doubt about it, Noah was from the same gene pool as Adam and Eve.

Think about it. Suppose God Almighty Himself stopped in your backyard one day to talk with you. Then suppose He told you He was about to destroy the whole neighborhood and save you and yours. Suppose He assigned you to do something you did not understand, and when you finally grasped it, it would be completely ridiculous. Wouldn't you have a few questions?

That is exactly what happened to Noah, minus the questions part. God talked to him about the end of the world, and Noah just stood there, nodding obediently at every word as if he understood everything being said to him. I could stand no more.

"Noah!" I shouted across the expanse, knowing full well no one would hear me. "This would be a good time to ask Him about the fine print. Get a little detail. Define some terms. Let me help you out. Let's start with the obvious, what do you say?"

I paced back and forth on my perch as I tried to coach Noah from afar. "Ask God what an ark is. Start right at the beginning."

If I didn't know what an ark was, which I did not, I was dead certain Noah did not have a clue; but did he ask for clarity? Not one bit. Noah stood there with no more understanding of what God was saying than if He had told him to build a barbeque pit for a neighborhood get-together.

Then God said to Noah, "I'm going to bring a flood on Earth that will destroy everything alive under heaven. Total destruction."

"Here's your chance, Noah," I coached from my perch. "Impress God with your intellectual curiosity. Ask Him what a flood is. He knows you have no idea what He's talking about. You've never even seen it rain."

God continued, "I'm going to establish a covenant with you. You will board the ship, and your sons, your wife, and your sons' wives will come on board with you. You are also to take two of every living creature, a male and a female, to preserve their lives with you: two of every species of bird, mammal, and reptile; two of everything so as to preserve their lives along with yours. Also, get the food you'll need, and store it up for you and them."

Several alarms should have gone off in Noah's head right then, but nary a ding-dong sounded. God's plan failed to consider the personalities involved. Noah should have pointed out a few things to Him. He should have said, "God, You haven't really been down here in quite a while. Things have changed. You can't imagine how complicated these people You've made have now become, especially the women.

"Let me explain the downside of this plan and what You're about to unleash if You put these people on an ark together. An ark must be a boat of some kind, right? A mother-in-law and her three daughters-in-law in one boat, full of wild animals?"

"And with no one to help out but Adam's grandsons," I would have added.

Noah should have waved his arms at this point for effect. "I mean really, Your Majesty, stop and think this through for a minute. Who is going to be in charge of what? Who gets kitchen duty versus potty patrol? Who is going to referee? It's not that I'm worried about the water, you understand. I am sure that I could survive Your flood if that's what You've got in mind for me. Believe me, I'm grateful, but You've got to know it's tenuous at best as to whether or not any of the men can survive the boat ride."

Noah had nothing close to the training needed to go into the boat-building business. Maybe that's why it took him so long to get it done. He should have asked God from the get-go how long this project was supposed to take. Once he began, it seemed to take forever. To be sure, people lived longer in those days. Noah was himself six hundred years old, so perhaps they were not subject to the hurry-up syndrome that would develop in future generations. No matter, the longer it went on, the more people talked.

Noah tried to do everything just as God told him. Unfortunately for Noah, God didn't mention anything about how the neighbors were going to react to a construction site and a petting zoo in the neighborhood. They complained loudly when they weren't laughing at the crazy old man next door. His family was so humiliated; they finally stopped leaving the house at all during daylight hours.

Then one day it started to rain. It rained, and still it rained. It rained so much that for the second time in its history, floodwaters were about to cover the earth. Let me tell you, the water came from everywhere. It came from above, and it came from below. It poured from the sky, and it sprang up like a geyser from beneath the surface of the planet. It was a flood all right, but oddly, it was not the same kind of flood as the one Lucifer had caused before Adam.

Lucifer's flood came from Earth itself as creation retched and rebelled against the demonic hostility that had ravaged it. Lucifer's flood was a response by creation to drown itself rather than endure the onslaught of Lucifer's horde. In Lucifer's flood, the seas left their banks and became hostile and a haven for the disembodied spirits who had fallen from heaven with the rest of us.

Noah's flood was not like that at all. Lucifer's flood rendered all of Earth empty and void. Noah's flood was water, but it was just water. What it would cover would emerge again in a viable form. The flood would not destroy Earth itself, only the breathing life upon it.

I watched as Noah and the kids, the kids-in-law, and all of those animals went into the ark as God Himself closed the door behind them. More than that, I watched the other people who stood around mocking Noah. Even as the rain fell, they remained unconcerned and completely unaware of what was about to happen to them. But when the waters rose above the roofs of their houses and the ark began to float, they began to call to Noah for help. Some swam toward the ark and might have latched on to it, but they were overrun and pushed down into the water by the Nephilim, who were intent on escaping the flood.

Being part human and part angel, the Nephilim were enormous and of great strength. They swam madly for the ark and climbed its outside walls, grabbing hold of the deck with their fierce clawlike hands. Noah and his sons fought them off by pounding their hands with hammers, forcing them to let go. The Nephilim were the very reason for the destruction of life upon Earth; they could not be allowed to escape the flood.

Soon all life would succumb to the waters, which covered Earth for one hundred fifty days. I sat on my perch for every one of them watching the ark. I could not stop thinking about why or how Noah had found favor with the Lord.

"Based on what?" I asked myself. "Of all the human possibilities, why was Noah singled out for such a purpose? When did Noah come to know God so well that he would sign on to such an outlandish plan? Noah must have had some doubt as to whether two of every kind of animal in the world would simply wander up to the ark and get in. He didn't even own a dog. He didn't know the first thing about taking care of wild animals, some of which were natural enemies; some were even prone to eat the others.

As I thought about how simple Noah was, I wondered whether or not he was God's first choice for the job. I watched humans all the livelong day. I knew how many there were and where they were, and I can tell you from my careful observation, there were other candidates who had it more together than Noah did. Whether or not God had spoken to anyone else about the job opening, I could not say since that whole interview process slipped right by us. But if He had, I suspect one or two of the other humans would have interviewed pretty well.

Right off the top, I could think of several engineers I had monitored in the past who had a lot of potential. Any of them would have had some good ideas for God. Certainly they would have been able to show Him how to make the construction process more efficient. In a one-on-one tussle of know-how and corporate ambition, Noah would have lost out against any of those guys who could have done the job in half the time. As I saw it, Noah was a poor choice and barely got the thing built before the rains came. Why did God choose him? What made him righteous? God spoke, and Noah obeyed. Could it really be that simple?

"Of course," I clicked my claws together and said aloud. "It's God's soft spot."

God was a soft touch when confronted with unquestioning obedience; He always had been.

Finally, on the seventeenth day of the seventh month the ark came to rest on the mountains of Ararat, and by the first day of the first month of Noah's six hundred first birthday, the water had almost completely dried up. Noah removed the covering from the ark, and by the twenty-seventh day of the second month, Earth was completely dry. God called them out, and Noah was so glad to be off that boat, he set up an altar and sacrificed an offering to God. You might know he would lock dead-on to God's other soft spot: worshipful gratitude. This pleased God so much that He went way over the top and spoke an incredible promise over Earth, which I was sure He would come to regret.

"I'll never again curse the ground because of people. I know they have this bent toward evil from an early age, but I'll never again kill off every living thing by a flood."

"God," I wanted to cry out, "will You listen to Yourself? This human experiment of Yours has fatal flaws. Don't get sentimental now. Retain your options. You know You will never put up with the evil that man is capable of conceiving."

I was getting so worked up I was tempted to fly right out there and confront God to His face.

"Remember how You completely overreacted to that pride business when You threw us out of heaven?" I would demand. "What? Now You're going to ignore all that man is sure to do to rebel against You in the future? Listen to what You just said. How could You promise such a thing? What can You possibly be thinking?"

I was mad at and felt bad for God at the same time. I knew such an impetuous display of love and hope like what had burst forth from Him was going to be a heartbreak later on. He had to know that it would only be a matter of time until mankind fell into rebellion again. Noah was old and now too dependent on the wine to hold out much hope for further exploits. His children held no great promise that I could see. One of them, Ham, well, let's just say that apple not only fell far from the tree, but also it rolled down the street to the next block.

The cold chill crawling up my spine alerted me that Satan had come close to my perch. I wished he wouldn't do that; my nerves were bad enough.

"Is the flood over?" he asked.

"Yes," I replied. "And it looks to me that God has made a tactical error that will make it more difficult for Him to deal with Earth in the future. Maybe He has no further plans for it after this generation."

"What about Og?" Satan asked.

"Og? What about him?" I had no idea why he was asking about the Nephilim king.

Enjoying my bewilderment, Satan condescended to tell me, "Og tried to hide in the rafters of the ark. I wonder if he made it."

CHAPTER 18

I'M SURE GOD was expecting more lasting results from the flood than what He got. It wasn't long until humans played right back into Satan's hands. I suppose God did manage to clean up the gene pool in both man and the animals, but beyond that, there was very little behavioral modification in the humans. I wondered what it would finally take for God to admit that the idea of free will was going to be a continual source of trouble for Him. Unless He pulled it out of the human formula, I could not see anything changing.

If you wanted to see a man hugging trees and kissing the ground, you should have been there when Noah stepped out on terra firma. He was so glad to be off that boat, he could not wait to start planting gardens. He didn't care what he planted; he just wanted to feel dirt in his hands. One crop that grew well for him was the grape. There were grapes all over the place, so many that no one family could eat them all. So naturally, Noah went into the wine-making business. The only problem was that he sampled so much of his product that he was always passing out.

Satan had told me to keep an eye on this situation in case Noah slipped up in some way. I obeyed, but I knew better.

"Not going to happen," I said to myself. "Noah might drink too much wine and drift off to sleep wherever he happens to be, but he isn't about to do anything to affect his standing with God."

I might have known Satan didn't really have any interest in Noah anymore. It was Ham upon whom he had his glassy eye. I knew the boy was going to be bait for the demons at some point. He, of all the kids, had been the one most intrigued by the sexual perversion that had been upon Earth. Noah never knew a thing about it, of course, but Ham found some of the goings on exciting to watch. As soon as Satan saw the opening in Ham's soul, he dispatched an earthbound spirit of lust and another of voyeurism to attach themselves to Ham. The weeks Ham spent on the ark with nothing but time on his hands had allowed a craving to develop deep inside him (fueled by the evil spirits' urgings) for the kind of excitement he used to enjoy in secret. He was such an easy mark. He didn't resist the temptation at all.

It happened one afternoon when Noah was sampling the wine, as was his custom. Tasting a few too many, which was also his custom, he wandered into his tent to sleep it off, another custom. Because of the warmness of the day, Noah usually took his clothes off and slept naked on his bed. I don't know how the door was left open on that particular day. Noah might have done it, or maybe Satan caused it to blow open, but however it came about, Noah lay unconscious, totally nude, when Ham passed by.

I should have known Satan had set the whole thing up when he called us together to watch and see what would happen. Ham's disdain for his father was well known and often gossiped about in the demonic ranks. Although it had been my assignment to watch Earth, because I didn't know about Noah until God selected him to rescue the human race, I completely missed whatever happened to breach the relationship between Noah and his son. So, although I had my own ideas, I didn't know for certain what the root of the offense had been. Some of the demons claimed to have seen what happened but did not think it important enough at the time to tell me. Because demons lie so often, it's foolish to rely on any information from them anyway. So I went with my own theory for Ham's character dysfunction: middle-child syndrome. That had to be it.

When Ham entered the tent, Satan sent a slew of spirits in after him: rejection, pride, and envy—all the usual suspects. Satan's eyes burned with satisfaction as he listened to Ham curse his father and make fun of his inebriated stupor.

Shem and Japheth were outside the tent when Ham came stumbling out. "What have you done?" they shouted as they grabbed him by the arm.

"Nothing. Leave me alone," he said as he tried to push his way past them.

"Tell me what you did." Shem held tightly to Ham's arm. "Why were you in his tent?"

"None of your business," Ham struggled to break free. "It was an accident. I didn't know he was in there."

Shem and Japheth did not buy into his story for a moment. They knew full well Ham would not hesitate to embarrass his father. They shoved Ham aside as they took a cloth and walked into the tent backwards to cover their father's nakedness without looking at him. But when Noah woke up and realized how Ham had disrespected him, you could have heard him screaming and cursing from any spot in the universe.

Since none of the boys were actually in the tent when Noah woke up, I found it amusing how Noah knew exactly which one had humiliated him. Before this happened, as a dad, Noah had ignored the rumors saying there was something perverse about Ham. It was obvious now that he knew better.

Satan, as you might expect, was beside himself with joy over this one. Ham would be the father of an entire nation whose sin would be passed down for generations. God knew about the brokenness in Ham and should have put a stop to his lineage right then and there. Why allow him to propagate? Ham was not a candidate for rehabilitation. If God let the bloodline continue, things could only get worse in future generations. And, of course, that is exactly what happened.

One of Ham's children was Cush, who had a son named Nimrod. This boy was bad even by our standards. He was a hunter, but not just of animals. He became a hunter of souls for Satan through his morbid fascination with the prince of darkness. Satan himself mentored Nimrod and even found the perfect wife for him.

Her name was Semiramis, and she fancied herself to be the high priestess of the demonic realm, if you can believe it. One really had to admire Satan's ability to seduce humans into thinking he would share his power with them. The grandiose lies Satan could conjure up to entrap mankind were bizarre and completely unbelievable; yet, they nearly always worked. More bizarre than the lies themselves were the humans who believed them in spite of all reason—all done in the human quest for spiritual power.

Satan told Semiramis she would become pregnant by a sunbeam. What is it with human women? She will demand written detail of the simplest thing a man might propose. How is it she will turn around and listen to Satan make the most outlandish claims and never think once to ask for a character reference? Semiramis actually believed what Satan said. She did become pregnant all right, but believe me, there was no sunbeam involved. It was Satan himself who planted his evil seed within her. She gave birth to a son named Tammuz. I remembered what God had said in the garden that day about Satan's seed, but I never really thought it would happen.

Tammuz was a hunter also, unfortunately for him; he wasn't very good at it. He managed to get himself killed by a wild boar. Semiramis went into mourning for forty days, and when she was done, she declared that Tammuz had come back to life. Of course, he hadn't, at least not the part of him that was human. But his demonic nature made a complete recovery. By this time, he and his mother were completely in the clutches of Satan.

If it had not been for Eve and how she filled in the missing gaps in Adam's personality, Satan would probably never have thought about how much there was to be gained by having women on the team. We had certainly never had any in our ranks before. But now here she was, Semiramis, the queen of heaven and the high priestess of Satan. She and her son, Tammuz, would seduce many into the worship of themselves, which they would turn to worship of Satan. Hard to believe humans could not see right through that charade, but most did not then and many of you do not now.

As the sons of Noah spread out over the entire earth, so the worship of Semiramis and Tammuz would cover the same land. Over time, they would be known by many names. It was because of Semiramis that Nimrod built a high place of worship intended to reach into second heaven. The human shell of Semiramis kept her bound to Earth, but her spirit and soul, being lost to her, longed for second heaven to be near Satan. To keep peace in the house, Nimrod built a temple for her. Satan was positively giddy with the prospect of an earthly temple connecting the demonic realm with Earth.

I must say it did look like the old serpent had them this time, but I still remained jittery about the whole thing.

"There is no way God will look the other way while His humans march headlong into perfect demonic possession," I remarked to a few of the demons who were hanging around my perch. Of course, they couldn't wait to tattle to Satan that I was a doomsayer.

"Look," Satan growled at them. "We had a wager, and I won. Just like I told Him, given free will, His miserable little humans would choose to worship me, and they did." Satan chuckled, "I don't see there is much He can do about it this time."

As I listened to Satan boast, I caught myself chewing on my claws. It is a terrible habit I picked up. I saw some of the humans doing it with their fingernails, and it seemed to calm them, so I thought I would give it a try. I can't say that it works that well, but once you get started, it's hard to stop.

I considered reminding Satan how his bragging against God was the very reason we were exiles. If he would keep quiet for once, perhaps God might not notice the tower going up.

Too late. Thunder rolled, lightning made a direct hit on the tower, and the whole thing collapsed into rubble just that quick.

"Can He do that?" Satan bellowed at me. He had never asked my opinion on anything before, so for a moment I was stunned and didn't answer.

"Is it illegal?" he snapped at me again.

"I—I don't know," I stammered.

"It's a violation of the rules. I want to talk to Him," Satan went on.

I took a quick peak over the edge to check out the collapsed structure before speaking.

"Uh, sir," I said haltingly, "I don't think God is in the mood to negotiate."

Satan and the others stood along the rim, stunned by what had happened to the people of Earth.

"How bad is it?" Satan asked.

"It looks like a total effect. God has completely confused their language. They cannot communicate."

"What about Semiramis?" he asked.

"There she is," I pointed out, "running around babbling like the rest of them." Satan took a swipe at me.

I have never seen the humans as confused and confounded as they were that day. One minute they were able to talk to each other, and the next moment they were all talking at once, but no one could understand a word the other was saying. It was chaos.

We were caught off guard because, as far as any of us could remember, God had never created chaos. It was brilliant when you think about it. No one was killed. No massive destruction; no floods, no fires, or other calamities; just utter and complete bedlam.

Of course, the humans quickly abandoned the building project. Semiramis and Tammuz were positively livid, but since no one could understand their ranting, the people simply wandered back to their own homes. Most were trying to figure out what had happened to them but had no idea whatsoever of the extraordinary supernatural event that had just taken place.

Satan insisted that God had broken the rules of engagement when He intervened directly into the affairs of Earth. Finally, one of our former demons had endured quite enough of Satan's incessant whining, and he screamed at Satan.

"He does what He does because He is who He is, and you will never win over Him. We were fools to follow you."

I said he was one of our former colleagues because, unfortunately for him, he no longer exists. Satan ate him.

CHAPTER 19

TIME KEPT MOVING with no regard as to how chaotic heaven and Earth had become. I thought God should have stopped the clock, reassessed how things were going, and let both sides regroup. Nothing like that happened. Time marched at its measured pace, and nothing could slow it down or speed it up.

Noah's sons continued to have kids, but none of them demonstrated any real promise of usefulness to God or in redeeming the confused mess reigning on Earth. God should never have bound Himself to getting things done on Earth through human beings and human beings alone. It was not working out.

It was not as if the humans were disinterested in finding God's will. In fact, we were amazed at how spiritual humans were since they were only made of flesh and blood. They could not see God, and they could not see us either, and yet they were completely convinced that some other rank of spiritual entity, as well as God, existed. They also seemed to be aware of a power structure in the spiritual world. Most of Earth people innately "knew" there was an all-powerful God out there somewhere. Most also believed this God was inaccessible to them, and so they sought intermediaries to be advocates between themselves and this God. Satan's strategy to seize this opportunity was brilliant.

Demons were assigned to humans so when the people petitioned "the gods," the demon on duty would respond. Here's how ingenious Satan's plan was. Say a person's child became ill. A parent begged the "god of the flu" to heal his child. Well, certainly a demon couldn't do anything of the kind unless the demon had made the child sick to start with. A demon could undo whatever he had done, but he could not do a creative miracle, such as healing someone.

That's how the demons became "gods" to them. They were always begging us to do things. Ironic, isn't it? Especially when you know the only lust Satan had for their kind was to devour them.

God, on the other hand, would not do tricks to prove He existed. The demons, however, would because it was so easy to snare them once we acted on a request to curse a neighbor or cause harm to an enemy. We were still bound by the rules of engagement and could not touch a human directly, but we could manipulate circumstances to get the desired effect. For example, we could not push someone over a ledge, but we could make sure there was a reason for a person to be on the ledge to start with.

With a little help from us, mankind soon learned some plants were hallucinogenic. When people ate them and chanted themselves into a lustful frenzy, we were right there encouraging them to abandon their natural inhibitions God had placed in them for their protection. Once they lost one, it was gone forever.

What with the drugs and our quickness to make them think they were in touch with some super power, humans were crazy in their desire to worship us. Satan found it thrilling, and I found it embarrassing, especially when they started imagining what we might look like. Somehow they got the ridiculous idea that we came from rocks. The stonecutters would carve outrageously bizarre little statues and declare they were idols made in the perfect images of the gods. The people wanted to buy the idols and take them home. Satan picked up on it right away. Humans wanted a god they could hold in their hands.

God would never have stood for such an abomination, but Satan did. The truth be told, it was downright insulting that anyone would think a powerful demon could be anything like one of those pathetic idols. As frightful as we might have been, we were much better looking than the way they depicted us. Satan, who himself is normally the essence of vanity, shook it off and said, "Worship is worship; take it where you find it." What amazed us was if humans truly believed we looked like those idols, why didn't they gasp and run?

Once the stonecutters convinced the masses that worshiping ugly rocks was a sane thing for rational people to do, it wasn't long until some figured out how to make a business out of religion. The one who had the largest franchise in idol making was a fellow named Terah. He was one of Shem's grandkids. Terah had shelves of every idol known to man and available in all prices. His business was booming.

Terah had a son named Abram. One fine day, Terah went to the market and left Abram in charge of the store. I didn't think much of it when it first happened. After all, I've seen a lot of teenage humans do silly things for no good reason. At first, I thought maybe one of the demons was having sport with the boy and had unleashed a spirit of destruction on him.

Later when I offered that as an explanation to Satan as to why I had not reported it sooner, he roared at me and called me an imbecile. He also told me not to think anymore. Anyway, quite suddenly, Abram took a broom from his father's closet and went about smashing every idol in the place.

When Terah came back to the store and saw what Abram had done, he was livid.

"Why did you do such a thing?" he yelled at the boy.

"Because, Father, if they were truly gods, shouldn't they have been able to defend themselves?"

Terah ranted, "Of course they are not gods. They have no power. They are only made of stone and metal."

Abram looked his father in the eye and said, "Father, do you realize what you have said?"

Whether or not Terah understood what he said was unimportant to us. Our eyes were now locked on the boy Abram. Something entirely new in the human race had surfaced: spiritual discernment. This could not be a positive development.

Right away I figured out what, or should I say who, was behind Abram's rampage, but I was not about to say a word because I did not want the grief. Not only did I know it was Ruah Ha Kadosh who had put the idea into Abram's head, but I also knew what was going to happen next. God was going to speak to Abram, no doubt about it, and it was just a matter of time until He did.

I had become pretty good at predicting when God was about to personally invade Earth's history, but I never was able to guess how. What new scheme would He come up with to try to save the humans from themselves? It always had to begin with a specific person. When I saw God pick out one of them for destiny, I would listen intently so as not to miss a word. Though, I must tell you, the human part of the conversation changed very little from Adam to Abram. When God suddenly appeared in their circumstances, not one of them showed surprise. I was certain none had ever talked with God before, so why did they behave as if the next-door neighbor had stopped over for tea? I postulated a theory, which if I were right, Satan would be beside himself in wrath. The humans had God's spiritual DNA. When God dropped in, He felt like family. I shuttered at what this might mean if they ever figured it out.

Decades later, God did stop by. Abram was no longer the upstart teenager. He had left those years far behind. In fact, he left behind a good bit of his adult years. Middle age was a distant image in the rearview mirror of his life.

God said to the elderly Abram, "Leave your country, your people, and your father's household, and go to the land I will show you."

Just like that.

Don't ask me how I knew. Just believe me; I knew without one doubt that Abram was going to obey. I saw it in Noah, and now I saw it in Abram: the uncanny willingness to believe what God says is true.

God saw it too, and He continued, "I will make you a great nation. I will make your name great, and all Earth will be blessed by you."

Then He went quite over the edge, as He was prone to do when someone has His favor.

"I will bless those who bless you and curse those who curse you."

Abram had not the slightest idea what had just been said, but Satan did. Oh, yes, when I told him, he understood it completely. If Abram obeyed, the human race was about to take a turn he had not counted on.

Satan wasted no time in sending the demon of doubt and unbelief to Earth to bombard Abram's mind with confusion.

"Ask Him for a map," the dark prince hissed in Abram's ear. "Make Him show you a deed. How long is this going to take? Ask Him for proof of performance. You are the heir of your father's fortune; you are a fool if you walk away from riches for a God whom you have never heard from before. If He is real, where has He been all this time?"

"Those are great questions," I cheered from heaven's rim. "You do it, Abram. Insist on an advance. Trust me, God doesn't have a backup candidate. Use your leverage."

But it did not work. Abram packed up the camels, the wife, and the nephew and set off as if he knew exactly where he was going. The prince went back in defeat to Satan's fury. I stayed and watched Abram's caravan disappear over the horizon.

Oh, how I wished I could have gone with him.

CHAPTER 20

I WATCHED THEM LEAVE and marveled at how unconcerned they seemed to be with how old they were. Abram was seventy-five years old, and his wife, Sarai, was sixty-five (or so she said—with women, who can be sure?) when they started off for the land of Canaan. It was as if marching off the map to an undiscovered country were a normal thing for two people to do who really ought to be thinking about retirement. Satan had made it painfully clear to me to stick close to them at all times so there would be no conversations with God without his knowing about it. When God showed up again to talk to Abram, I would hear every word of it.

It was several weeks before the Lord appeared to Abram again. I knew by now how God could show up anywhere and at any time with no warning, so I was not surprised when He encountered Abram in the middle of the day in the middle of the road. Abram, on the other hand, having talked to God only one other time in his life, was not accustomed to such a strange encounter, and neither was his camel who bleated in fear, threw Abram off, and ran away with Abram chasing behind. I suppose it was God who stopped the animal so Abram could catch up.

Abram was sweating and breathing hard as he waited to see what God would say. "Look around," He said to Abram. "To your offspring I will give this land."

Just like Noah had done when he got off the boat, Abram's first response to God was not to ask a few good *when* and *how* questions; rather, he halted the whole caravan and built an altar to God right there in the traffic lane. With gratitude for what he had not yet received, Abram worshiped as if there were no doubt about God's truthfulness.

But Abram didn't stop there. He moved on to Bethel, and he built an altar. Everywhere they stopped to spend the night, Abram built an altar. The caravan was making terrible time because of the unscheduled stops, but you can guess how it pleased God. From that point on, Abram could do no wrong in God's eyes. Not only did the altar building positively guarantee Abram's success, but it also meant bad news for Satan. Before the altars were built, he had reigned and reveled in each of those locations without the slightest resistance. Just as soon as the altars went up and Abram declared that God was Lord over that place, the land trembled, and Satan felt his hold weaken. Although in nine million years he would never have admitted to such a thing, we knew it was so.

That was not the worst of it by far. Oh, my, no. The worst was right around the corner; a full-frontal assault on Satan's tactics in a way he had not anticipated. Abram started to pray. No one had truly prayed before.

To be sure, the demons knew that when humans get into trouble or get scared, they are likely to start crying out to some hoped-for cosmic rescuer in the sky. Begging for help is not the same thing as praying. Begging, wailing, and groveling did not constitute a petition to God. It was more yelling for help to any celestial being within earshot who might respond to the person's promises to live better in the future if only rescued from his circumstances in the now.

You humans still do this, although you still do not seriously expect anyone to answer, and generally speaking, no one does. As long as mankind confused *pleading* with *praying*, the issue of prayer was of no concern to Satan. That's why at first he seemed so disinterested in my report.

"So he's praying," Satan said without looking up from what he was doing. "So what?"

"It's not what you think, master." I tried to explain that the kind of prayer coming from Abram was different and much more serious than any version of prayer previously known to be in the spiritual skill set of humanity.

"Different? How?" Satan replied. "And don't waste my time."

"Abram is actually talking to God. He's thanking God for His mercy and protection on behalf of his family, his friends, his servants, the camels, the camel drivers, the dogs, and the cats. Abram is leaving nothing and no one uncovered." I wasn't sure I was getting through.

Satan had never before worried about the kind of whiny, wimpy prayer he was accustomed to hearing from you humans. He had often said that mankind's constant complaining to God was likely to have been more annoying to Him than helpful.

"Abram's prayer is nothing like you've heard before," I insisted.

"OK, so the old man's prayer is different. Tell me why I care." At least he was paying attention to me.

"It's…it's," I waved my hands around as if trying to pull the word I was looking for out of thin air. "It's intercession. That's what it is."

"So, it is prayer, then." He seemed annoyed. "Prayer has never helped them."

"That's because no human has ever engaged in intercession." I tried to make him see the urgency of the situation.

"Never?" Satan asked as if trying to remember if he knew of such a thing.

"We would have been the first to know if it had ever happened anywhere on Earth. Whining, begging, groveling, pleading, bargaining, trying to make a deal—all the time; but intercession? Never." I was exhausted from my attempt to warn him.

Satan's hordes were highly skilled in blocking mankind's prayer attempts, so Satan was simply not troubled by what I had to say.

"Earth people think prayer is about explaining situations to God, which He already knows and understands far better than they do." Satan responded. "You know how the demons look forward to human prayer if it's a slow day."

He was right; it was like a game to them. Desperate people released their prayerettes, void of any direction, power, or authority. The little prayers floated up toward God all right, but first the fragile petitions had to pass through second heaven, where the demons shot them down before they came close to getting to God. I didn't know exactly what the repercussions of intercession might be, but I was certain there would be nothing fun about it.

I tried to explain it better. "Human prayers are like wishes floating toward heaven. Sometimes they get there, sometimes they don't, but nobody expects an answer anyway. Intercession doesn't involve wishing. It is directive and rapid. It declares what God has promised and demands it come about. It insists God remember what He has said and act upon it."

Satan looked perplexed, so I decided to chance going further. "What is more, God likes intercession."

He still wasn't getting it, so I tried harder. "God has tried for centuries to get His people to engage Him, command Him concerning His words, so to speak. Someone is finally doing it."

Satan did not believe me until he experienced it for himself. Before he could say another word, a blast of lightning broke through the stone floor in front of him, knocked him back, and then crashed through the ceiling above.

"What happened?" he demanded as he righted himself.

"That's it! That's what I've been trying to tell you. It's Abram's intercession."

We were soon to learn how intercessory prayers could speed through second heaven so quickly and with such force, the demons would have to dance a jig to avoid being hit by one. Satan, who before had feared nothing mankind might do, hopped like a bunny right along with the rest of us to avoid getting in the path of intercession. Once intercession began, the prayers came in such a rapid-fire rhythm that they tore gaping holes in the floor and left the demons dazed and confused about where to stand to avoid being hit by the next one.

As Abram got better at intercession, it became worse for us. As fast as intercession went up, the response came hurling back even faster. I cannot tell you how many a demon could not get out of the way fast enough and was flattened by an incoming answer from heaven. While we were looking at the floor, trying to guess where the next one was likely to come through, Adonai would be up there slamming the answers back down faster, and all the better if it sideswiped one of the demons on the way. Why, sometimes a tail or a wing was cut right off. When intercession started, we couldn't get out off the way fast enough.

Then it got worse yet for Satan. When God cleaned up the seas at the restoration of Earth, the spirits who had been confined in the dank waters were evicted and had nowhere to go, so they floated aimlessly about the planet until the Fall of man in the garden. After that, if a human gave one an opening, the spirit could set up a habitation with the soul of the human. For example, Ham opened the door of his soul to a perverse spirit as a result of his preoccupation with the Nephilim. That's why a spirit of perversion plagued Ham and his descendants forever.

By Abram's time, it was commonplace for spirits to be clustered and deeply embedded in human souls. But once intercession started, the spirits could not be depended upon to hold their position. When the first prayer assault launched, the terrified spirits started flying out of the human bodies they inhabited. Like a buzzing cloud of bees, they came swarming toward second heaven, where Satan and the demons swatted madly at them, trying to shoo them back to Earth and hurling threats to destroy them if they did not return. Although the spirits knew Satan would make good on his threat for having left their human hosts, faced with a choice between the wrath of Satan and the wrath of God, the evil spirits took their chances against Satan.

Well, you can imagine the problems this meant for Satan when humans were suddenly freed from the spirits who had controlled their behavior. It became almost impossible to manipulate the people through the weakness in their natures any longer. I tell you, it was a mess. From that day till this, Satan will do almost anything to keep intercession from beginning. I would never want to be quoted, but I can tell you that I have personally known high-ranking demons to cut and run before facing a fight with intercessors.

Not trusting me to handle it myself, Satan assigned an entire contingent of demons to stand watch over Abram's progress. We kept watching and hoping for an opportunity to intervene in Abram's journey and distract him from praying. When we found none, I was the one—as was always the case when there was bad news—who had to report it to Satan.

"Solve this problem," Satan snarled at me. "Stop him."

"Sir," I stammered, "you know the rules. We cannot do it if we cannot find a human to be our agent."

I knew he didn't want me to remind him, but it was the rules of engagement thing; Satan had to get things done on Earth through human beings, just like God. If he could not enlist one, he could not interfere with the events of Earth.

"Abram must have enemies," Satan retorted.

"He does, sir, but God has made them afraid of him. He's golden. They won't challenge him."

Satan ordered me back, ignoring the problem and demanding results.

We kept watching, hoping someone would be willing to move against Abram. We thought we had a few good candidates along the way, like the time Pharaoh lusted after Sarai. Now that right there convinced me Sarai probably lied about her age. But then who can explain the chemistry of attraction? Maybe it was the older-woman thing that attracted Pharaoh; whatever, but he really seemed intent on seducing her.

It looked like this might be the human agent we needed to get to Abram, but just when we thought we had him at the crucial point, Pharaoh was like the others who had backed off in fear of Abram. Maybe it wasn't Abram himself that struck them with fear. In fact, I doubt it was. It was the holy armor God had placed around Abram in response to all that altar building. No one else could see it except for us, but it worked really well. The curses and arrows the demons shot at him simply fell to the ground. I cannot tell you how much ammunition was wasted trying to take Abram out.

Satan summoned us back to his throne room to berate us for our failure to stop Abram's advance.

"His enemies won't touch him," one of the others spoke.

"Then work through his friends," Satan snapped back.

"I tell you, there's no opening," one demon blurted out before he thought about the consequences of challenging Satan's orders. Just as Satan was about to lash out at the demon who had unwisely spoken, I had an idea.

"Wait, maybe there is someone else."

"Who?" Satan asked.

"His nephew. Remember that spat with Cain and Abel and how much trouble it created for generations? Family feuds are simply wicked. What if Lot could be stirred against his uncle? Abram would never see it coming."

"Lot is the weak link," Satan said, beginning to take credit for my idea. "We'll stir up jealousy and resentment in Lot. Abram won't see it coming."

"Isn't that what I just said?" I coughed as I swallowed the words.

Satan knew timing was everything in making this work, so he restrained himself and the demons until he decided Lot was ripe. I thought he had waited too long. He should have moved earlier, before things got so good for them. But Satan seemed to think there was an advantage to letting Abram and his nephew get richer and richer.

"Why would Lot challenge Abram now, when everything in the world is going his way and he is in need of nothing?" I asked one of the others.

I tell you, Satan is a strategist. He anticipated that Abram would be able to take wealth in stride, but Lot would not. He waited until Lot was puffed up to the max and then dispatched the demon most skilled in planting resentment right to Lot's tent. When Lot went to sleep, the demon spoke into his dreams.

"You know what they're saying about you, Lot. How you can't hold your own. You'd never make it without your uncle watching your every step. He doesn't respect you either. He let's you think you're his partner, but he doesn't trust you with one sheep. Show him what you're made of. Demand your half now. Go your own way. Show them all."

It worked like the proverbial charm. It was just a few days until I heard Lot complain to one of the camel drivers about how his flocks didn't have enough grazing room because they were crowded by Abram's animals.

Lot didn't seem to notice the quizzical look on the camel driver's face because, as everyone knew, all the flocks were Abram's.

With the demon's encouragement, Lot finally worked himself into full-blown resentment toward the man who was his benefactor. He was belligerent and rude as he approached Abram and demanded half of the herds.

"Lot is trying to negotiate a departure settlement with Abram," I breathlessly reported to Satan. "You were right. He wants to go out on his own, so he's trying to broker a deal between the animals he acquired versus the ones belonging to Abram. Can you stand it?" I was so excited.

Satan laughed at the easy target Lot had been. Satan's hordes as well as Abram's army knew Lot had no legitimate claim to anything Abram owned. Lot was a hanger-on, a wannabe who never was. His sole redeeming feature was his blood link to Abram.

In the end, Abram told Lot that he could choose the land he wanted for his flocks and herds and that Abram would take what was left. Satan was especially perplexed by Abram's actions. There was no way he could process the concept of generosity.

"Why is he doing it?" Satan asked.

"Lot has always been a drag on the family business," I offered. "Maybe it's worth it to Abram to be rid of him."

The two men parted company, and Lot chose for himself the whole plain of the Jordan and set out toward the east. Abram settled in the land of Canaan, while Lot chose to live among the cities of the plain and pitched his tents near Sodom. More good news for Satan. I couldn't wait to tell him.

"Sodom? Near Gomorrah?" he couldn't believe it. "You're kidding. Abram's nephew is moving into our backyard?"

I nodded, thrilled that now twice in a row I had reported something to Satan that didn't end with me being blamed for it. Not since the heyday of the Nephilim had there been a pit of unrestrained degradation as there was in Sodom. It was a playground for the worst of us.

Under different circumstances, the demons might have turned their attention immediately to Lot and made quick sport of him. It would have been laughable to suppose for a moment that Lot might have had the moral character to withstand what Satan had going on down in Sodom and Gomorrah. It would only be a matter of time until one way or the other Lot would be swept up into the perversion.

"Let's do it," one of the demons sneered, licking his lips at the prospect. "Let's go for Lot."

Lot would have been so easy, but Satan wouldn't give it the time of day. He wasn't interested in Lot. Lot was not worth his time, but Abram was. Only Abram had the potential to bring forth the promise God made to Satan in the garden—the one about the offspring of the woman crushing Satan's head. I couldn't imagine why Satan was still worried about that happening. Now Abram was over eighty years old, and Sarah was over seventy if she was a day. Their biological clocks stopped ticking decades ago, and surely they were too old to adopt.

Satan had a renewed interest in Lot when he figured out how to use him to lure Abram into a snare. Satan stirred up a battle between the kings of Sodom and Gomorrah and the other four kings in that region. Sodom was overrun by the invading kings who ransacked the city and carried off all the assets, including the people, who included Lot.

One of the survivors of this battle reported to Abram what had occurred, so, naturally, Abram gathered his men together and went after Lot. Abram caught up with the raiding kings, and a fierce battle ensued. If numbers meant anything at all, Abram should have lost the battle. Satan counted on it. But Abram did not lose. In fact, he won it smashingly. It was the halo effect of all that altar building, I was sure of it.

Satan stomped and grumbled at his failed plan. I tried to explain to him why Abram was never going to lose in battle, but he didn't care to hear nor did he care to stay around for Abram's victory party, so he went back to his lair to pout. I went back to my perch and continued to watch Abram. It was a good thing I did.

CHAPTER 21

I F I HAD gotten there ten seconds later, I would never have seen the stranger come from nowhere to right in front of Abram. *Poof!*

Suddenly, he was gone, I think. But where did he go? I saw him; then I could not see him.

"I know he was a man," I reasoned to myself. "But a man cannot step in and out of reality like that, can he? Of course not; but he had to be a man. What else could he have been?"

Then he was back again—a strange, mysterious sort, different from anyone I had seen on Earth before. I heard him say his name was Melchizedek and that he was the king of Salem. Then he brought out bread and wine and shared it with Abram. He told Abram he was a priest and then said, "God the Most High Creator of heaven and Earth has blessed you, Abram, and defeated your enemies by your hand."

Abram was overcome by the moment and pledged to give him a tenth of everything he owned.

"Priest of God Most High?" I asked myself as I started winging it back toward Satan's den to tell him about it. "I don't think so. No way could there be a priest of God on Earth who somehow escaped our notice. King of Salem? Where is that, and, for that matter, what is a priest?"

I no more than got the words "king of Salem" out of my mouth before Satan ran right over the top of me and raced toward the rim to take a look. I dusted myself off and went after him, but by the time we got there, this priest or king, whatever he was, had disappeared.

Satan glared at me, "What did he say to Abram?"

"Really, sir, not all that much." I tried to calm him down. "He gave Abram some bread and wine. Then he left. Nothing more to it."

"You are certain?" He moved in closer to me, causing me to shrivel up a little bit.

"No, nothing," I said before I remembered the 10 percent item. I modified my response. "Nothing of importance."

Satan continued to glare at me with those awful eyes until I blabbed out the whole story.

"He blessed Abram and gave him bread and the wine, like I said." I sucked in my breath and spoke quickly.

"Then Abram promised to give him one-tenth of everything he owned, and that was it. End of story." I ducked just in case.

I certainly did not expect such insignificant information to send the prince of darkness into such a fit, but it did. He rambled and bellowed incoherently about an illegal visit from Adonai, then he shook his clawed fist toward God's heaven and raged about economics.

"Do you understand what this means, imbecile?" He yelled at me as I tried to crawl out of his way. I knew he didn't want an answer, so I cowered there in front of him, waiting until he got over himself. He grabbed me by the wing and stood me up in front of his distorted face.

"It means Abram will get richer and more powerful," he growled.

I nodded in agreement, though I couldn't make the connection in anything he was saying. To me, it didn't seem quite the same as when Adam and Eve gave some of their produce to God as an offering. How was giving a tenth of his wealth away to another human going to make Abram richer and more powerful? If anything, it meant he would have less, but I was not about to imply that Satan didn't know basic math. When I said nothing, he threw me down and strode into the darkness.

I continued to watch Abram and his family, but unless something really noteworthy occurred, I kept the day-to-day matters to myself. Wouldn't you know something noteworthy was right around the corner?

Abram was on a twilight stroll around the campground when God showed up again. "Do not be afraid, Abram. I am your shield and your very great reward."

Unlike their other encounters in which Abram's part was to nod and build altars, this time Abram had apparently been giving some thought to what God had promised Him so long ago.

"It's about time," I thought. "Abram has a few questions."

"O sovereign Lord," he began, "what can You give me since I remain childless and the one who will inherit my estate is Eliezer of Damascus?" Abram glanced up to see if God was listening, then he continued. "You have given me no children, so a servant in my household will be my heir."

I had wondered if Abram would get the nerve to bring it up to God that he was way too old to father anything, especially a nation, like God had promised him. As for Sarai, forget about it. She lost interest long ago. I was anxious to hear how God was going to answer.

God said, "A son coming from your own body will be your heir."

Abram looked down at his body. I also looked at his body, and I can tell you that it was not an inspiring sight. The Lord's plan was for Abram to impregnate Sarai.

"Come on, God," I thought to myself. "Admit it's too late. Come up with a consolation prize."

That is exactly what I expected Abram would say, but he didn't. Instead, Abram believed God—again—and God credited it to him as righteousness.

There it was again: believing God. Noah had done it and found favor with the Lord. Abram did it, and he was credited with righteousness. I tried to reason out what this meant. How does it work?

I paced back and forth on my perch and debated with myself. "If a human tells God he believes something that cannot possibly be true, does it win favor with God?"

"No, probably not," I answered my own question.

It has to be something more, but it could not be too hard or humans would never figure it out. Maybe it is like a game.

"That's it, and I'll bet Adonai is behind it," I thought, remembering His outlandish sense of humor.

Here is how the game most likely works. God proposes the most preposterous scheme possible—something that cannot possibly happen—and asks a human to believe it is true. Now, the human must say he believes it to be true even though it is contrary to his prior experience and in the absence of verifiable evidence.

To win the game, the human must not only *say* he believes what God has said, he must also start to *behave* as if he believes it. When he takes some sort of risky action to prove he's on board, bingo, God delivers on His promise, no matter how impossible it seemed or how much ruckus He must cause to make it happen.

Then I wondered, "But what happens if God speaks to a human who ignores Him?"

I already knew the answer to that question because I had seen it happen many times. In fact, most times. God would speak, and if no one responded, He simply moved on to the next person in line until He found someone who would react to Him. No wonder it takes God so long to get anything done on Earth. He has limited Himself to working with humans. He cannot do a thing until He finds one who will believe that "He is" and that He has spoken a promise to him or her. As soon as that happens, without fail, God disappears and may not show up again for years.

Naturally, this really perplexes human beings. The person with the promise must continue to believe it will come about no matter how long it takes or how unlikely it seems. The man or woman in question must continue to believe when others have stopped.

"How many humans could there be who can trust God like that?" I wondered.

Not many, I was sure. I didn't know whether to laugh at their simplicity or admire the ones who could step out and believe God with such certainty.

"Believe the impossible from a voice you cannot audibly hear, from a person you cannot physically see, and call it God?" I mused. "Then spend your life waiting for God to prove Himself. Trust God? Believe God? There must be another word for it."

CHAPTER 22

BRAM DIDN'T HAVE to say a thing. As soon as he came back from his evening stroll and opened the flap to the tent, Sarai knew something was up. When she looked at her husband's face, she knew he had been with God again. She had been nagging Abram for months to try to get another meeting, get a few specifics as to how and when all of His great promises were supposed to come about. Excited to see something had happened and eager to find out what God had said to her husband, she began to pry the information out of him.

Poor old Abram, so completely unaware of the havoc about to be unleashed in his life. I almost felt sorry for him. Anyone who understands women—anyone who has ever had a conversation with a woman—could have seen this problem with Sarai coming and would have run. But not Abram; he was completely clueless.

"What's for dinner?" he asked as he laid his staff aside and took off his sandals.

"And so? How did it go?" she asked while pouring out a cool drink.

"Fine," Abram answered. "What's for dinner?"

"First tell me what He said."

"He said you were going to have a baby. Are we eating out?" Abram continued as he lifted the covers off of several pots, wondering why he didn't smell anything cooking.

"And you said to Him what exactly?" Sarai was no longer pouring a drink or making any move that had to do with food.

"I didn't say anything. What's to say?" Abram, sensing this was going to be a long talk, began looking around for a scrap of bread or cheese.

"What's to say?" Temperature rising, nostrils flaring; yes, all the signs of a coming storm were clearly there. Her voice was beginning to take on that shrill sound.

"What's to say, old man? Nothing at all crossed your mind?" Sarai walked around the table and got in Abram's face.

"I don't know; maybe you could have said something like, 'Oh, Lord, how is this going to be? Have You noticed that my beloved Sarai is past the time of child-bearing?'"

Spotting a piece of bread behind the water jar, he reached for it, but she was not about to let him get away. Inserting herself between him and any type of food, she continued.

"How about something like this?" Sarai adjusted her head covering and folded her hands. "'Oh, Lord, maybe I misunderstood. My hearing isn't what it used to be with my age and all. What was that promise again?'"

Unfolding her hands and planting them firmly on her hips, she waited for Abram to respond.

"It will work out as He has said," Abram replied, reaching around her for the bread.

"Really, my husband? What a relief. I am so glad to know that you and I alone are about to defy the laws of time. A lesser person with the slightest idea about where babies come from would like a few more details about how such an extraordinary thing will come about, but not you." She was pacing back and forth in a high state of agitation by now.

"Sarai, He is God, not me. Am I to question Him? It has gone well with us because I have not doubted Him."

"Tell me exactly what He said, and don't leave anything out. You were never one for details."

"All right, already," Abram began. "He said to me, 'Your servant will not inherit your legacy, but a son coming from your own body will be your heir.' That is all there is to it."

Sarai's face looked suddenly suspicious.

"What more do you want?" Abram asked as he checked the cooking pots again to be sure he had not missed something.

"He said nothing about me?"

"Of course He said something about you. You are going to have a baby. What else do you want?" He gulped down the last of his drink.

"He said I was going to have a baby—exactly?" She pressed. "Try to remember."

"He said exactly I would have a son of my own loins. Of course you are going to have a baby. How else would I get a son?" Starving by now, Abram put on his sandals and went to the camel driver's tent in hopes that dinner was still being served.

Oh, if only Abram could have observed the behavior of human women for a few centuries as I had, he would have known never to deliver that kind of information to a woman and then leave her alone to process it. Why, the next four thousand years of human history might have been different if Abram had just a little insight into how women think. God should have warned him about how complex human women are. Personally, I think God Himself didn't always know quite what to expect from females. If the truth be known about it, God probably looked at women and wondered how one of His really clever ideas had become so much more complicated than He intended.

Nothing could have pulled me away from my perch right then; I did not want to miss the action I knew was coming. I could have written the script for what was about to take place in Sarai's mind. Women think men don't want to take the responsibility for anything, so they must take the responsibility for everything. It all started with Eve.

Remember back there in the garden when Adam told God that he had eaten of the forbidden fruit because Eve made him do it? God didn't buy his story for a minute. The words Adam spoke, pathetic excuses that they were, still had an unexpected and lasting effect on Eve and her daughters.

I don't think God anticipated how female reasoning would go askew the way it did. Remember, there were no females in heaven. There was no prototype. The whole experiment with women was an entirely new idea. Women have always been very complex.

Men, on the other hand, are not complex. Men are simply made with a standard emotional package; no frills, no fuss, nothing fancy like there is with women. Men have a basic range of emotions and a standard vocabulary through which they process life. This should have been the normal equipment in all humans, male and female, nothing more or less. Men understand up/down, left/ right, good/bad, black/white, hungry/eat, itch/scratch, tired/sleep, mad/yell, hit, grunt. Like that, you see? Easy and simple, that's the way it is with men.

Adam thought there were only two possible states of time: day or night. Eve insisted on breaking time into first light, dawn, morning, noon, afternoon, dusk, evening, night, just after midnight, and just before dawn.

And let me tell you about the colors. That was worse. Adam would say black or white. But Eve would say charcoal, ebony, deep black, barely black. And of course there was not just white. There was bone, eggshell, vanilla, ivory, pale white, glossy white—I could go on and on.

See what I mean? Now take that same propensity to make things more complex than they need to be and carry it into the emotional makeup of women.

Men get mad. Women get irritated, hurt, disappointed, annoyed, miffed, piqued, ruffled, upset, enraged—like that.

Here's how God had a good idea for everybody but failed to foresee how differently it might function between men and women. He put into humans a sense of shame and guilt, intended as a safety valve for their protection, so that when they turned from Him or sinned, the valve would trigger and they would feel something inside of themselves that convicted them of their error. Smart, right?

It was a simple job to install it into the soul of men. But when He started to put it into women, He had to work around the intricate wiring of those accessories and upgrades on the female model. God simply tightened the screw too much in the shame and guilt area. So, ever since Eve, if a man suggested to a woman that something might be her fault, she immediately thought that it was.

Adam said Eve made him eat the fruit. If you could have seen the size of him and the size of her, you would see how ridiculous that was. But in Eve's mind, because of that shame and guilt screw being too tight, her natural conclusion was, "Maybe I did. It must be my fault." A case of an overdeveloped sense of responsibility resides in every female who has ever been, because as I see it, God will not own up to the miscalculation and fix it.

It's that kind of dysfunctional reasoning that has stayed in Eve's daughters all the way to the present generation. And don't think for a moment that men haven't figured it out.

Therefore, when Abram repeated to Sarai what God had said to him, she analyzed the sentence structure. As I have seen women do time after time, she came to a logical and yet completely wrong conclusion about what God meant. Abram had been promised a son from his own body, but she had not. The Lord had intentionally not said anything about her.

"That must be it," she thought. "I'm too old to be the natural mother. I bet they talked about it and Abram doesn't want to tell me. He knows it will hurt my feelings. I must sacrifice my own desires. I must do something to see that Abram has an heir as God has said."

And that is when Sarai came up with one of the worst ideas in human history. She decided on her own to save the day. She believed she was too old to have children, but she had an Egyptian maidservant named Hagar who was not.

When Abram came back to the tent later that night, Sarai was waiting for him. "My husband, we must talk."

"Must we talk now?" he asked, full of bread and wine, desiring nothing more than to lie down.

"It has to be now; your happiness depends on it."

Having never heard her say anything close to this before when he had come home late, Abram came to attention. "What do you mean—my happiness?" He tried to remember if Sarai had ever been concerned about his happiness before.

Sarai sighed and said, "The Lord has kept me from having children."

"But so, who cares? You will have a baby now. The Lord said so." Abram tried to console her. "Now, let's go to bed." He turned as if going to lie down.

"No, my husband," she sighed even deeper.

Abram knew this conversation was going to happen no matter what, so he sat down on a pillow and motioned for her to go ahead.

"He said *you* would have a son. He said nothing about me. I am too old. I've thought it over. Go and sleep with my maidservant; perhaps I can build a family through her."

Now Abram, with that basic emotion package and simple thinking feature common to man, quite naturally thought that when Sarai proposed her preposterous idea, she must actually mean it. Which, of course, she thought she did at first.

When Sarai suggested Abram have sex with Hagar in order to secure an heir "from his own body," as God had promised, there were any number of ways Abram should have responded. Any of them would have been better than what he did.

He was supposed to gasp at the thought. He was supposed to fall down on his knees in gratitude when he realized how Sarai was willing to sacrifice her own happiness for his. He was supposed to marvel at how unselfish she was and how she was willing to put aside her own desperate desire for a child to secure his happiness. The number one thing in the top ten things that Abram was supposed to have done and did not: he was supposed to say, "No. Absolutely not. Inconceivable. Wouldn't consider it. The matter is settled. Don't mention it again."

He was supposed to say that having a child with another woman was unthinkable. He was supposed to say that he would never agree to such a thing. He was supposed to say they would wait and believe God until they died rather than have Sarai displaced by someone else.

What he did say was never, ever, not in ten thousand years what he was supposed to say: "OK, if you think so, dear."

My, oh, my, and I had thought Satan's wrath was awful. I had never seen a woman turn that color before. The fury that rose in Sarai's eyes made my wings wilt. Abram had no idea what he was in for. In fact, the whole human race would pay for the wrath of that woman scorned.

Abram slept with Hagar, and she conceived. Then the trouble really started. When she learned she was pregnant, Hagar began to despise Sarai. Do you wonder why? History has it wrong about this part of the story in that it blames Hagar for something she had absolutely no control over. It was bad enough for the young woman to find herself the paramour for a man old enough to be her grandfather's grandfather. It was no secret why she was in this position. The whole caravan knew the story. Sarai had insisted upon it. Now that Hagar was pregnant, she was angry with Sarai for causing a set of circumstances from which Hagar could never escape. Hagar's future was toast. When Sarai heard that Hagar was angry, Sarai got mad that Hagar was mad about being pregnant.

Then Sarai said to Abram, "You are responsible for the wrong I am suffering. I put my servant in your arms so that you could have your promised heir, and what do I get for my trouble? Now that she knows she's pregnant, she despises me. Look at what you've done."

Abram stood there scratching his head and trying to figure out why everyone was mad at him. Being a man, he thought Sarai would get over it once she remembered how the whole thing started. Not a chance.

"What I've done?" Abram asked. "Love of my life, I only did this for you. Isn't this what you wanted? Wasn't this your idea? We're going to get a baby and a nanny to boot. Isn't it great how it's working out?"

She hurled a clay pot at his head. This went on for about an hour, and at the end of it all, Abram told Sarai to do whatever she wanted with Hagar.

"Your servant is in your hands," Abram said. "Do with her whatever you think best."

Sarai took out her frustration on Hagar, who finally ran away, out into the desert alone. Hagar was scared to death and cried like a baby as she left with barely enough sustenance to keep her alive for a few days. Hagar had not been gone long before Sarai began to think it over, and, as I could have predicted, she started moving toward that guilt thing again.

"I was too hard on her," Sarai thought to herself. "Why wouldn't she hate me? She's just a child herself. She didn't want a baby with that old goat. Hagar didn't have any say in this matter. We forced her to do it. I feel badly that her mother had plans for her to marry one of the camel drivers next year. Of course, there's no chance for that now. Poor thing, out there in the desert. Lost and alone, I know she must be scared to death. This is all Abram's fault."

I couldn't be sure what God intended to do about all of this, but I knew Him well enough to know that He wouldn't let that young girl wander around out there in the desert, especially since she was pregnant with Abram's child. I knew it was God who brought about Sara's mind change, so it was a pretty safe bet He would send one of the angels to tell Hagar everything would be OK and to return to her mistress.

Not knowing about Sarai's change of heart or God's intervention with the angel, when Abram saw Hagar returning to the camp, all he could imagine was a lot of screaming and flying objects. He was certain Sarai would come out throwing pots with both hands. Imagine his surprise when Sarai emerged from the tent, ran past him, and welcomed the girl back with outstretched arms.

Oh, the hugs, and the "I'm sorry, so am I," kiss, kiss—it was enough to make a demon nauseous.

Sarai wrapped Hagar in her shawl and shepherded the girl into her very own tent. As they passed by Abram, who had no idea what had just happened, both women snarled at him.

"What did I do?" he asked no one in particular. He shrugged and started back for the tent just in time to see his pillow and mat come flying out the door, landing in the dust in front of him. From inside the tent, he could hear the sobbing of Hagar as she poured out her heart to Sarai, who clucked about her like an old hen with an orphan chick.

Abram considered barging into the tent and ordering both women to shape up, then throwing Hagar out of his tent to regain his standing with Sarai. Doing a quick mental inventory of the number of clay pots he supposed might still be in there, he thought better of it and set off to find someone to sympathize with him.

Abram went out to the desert and sat on a rock and cried to God, "God, where are You? What has happened to me? Why am I sleeping on a rock? I was thrown out of my own tent. Sarai hates me. Hagar hates me. Why did You let this happen?"

Now, I can tell you I was dumbfounded when God answered him. He just doesn't do that. He doesn't respond to whining. Usually, He doesn't give the whiner any attention at all. I was surprised when I heard Him answer Abram, "I did not tell you to be with Hagar."

"But it was Sarai's idea. It never crossed my mind to do such a thing."

"Oh, please," God interrupted. "Remember to whom you are talking. I know your every thought before you think it."

"But what am I going to do now? They have sided against me."

"Yes, I see that. Actually, I was afraid that might happen. The sisterhood bonding mix I put into women is a very delicate formula."

"You know, Mighty One ever to be praised," Abram whimpered, "I don't want to seem ungrateful. Thank You for the camels and the flocks and for saving Lot and all that, but it looks to me like most of the misery of life could have been avoided if You had not made women so complicated. Did You not declare how man was going to rule over her? You did say that, right? When is that part supposed to kick in?"

"Of course I said it, but it was not part of My plan A," God replied. "It was simply a statement as to how men would mistreat women if Eve followed Adam. Men ruling over women is the consequence of poor choices. I meant for them to rule together. But never mind, I intend to remedy that situation a little further down the timeline."

"I appreciate that You're thinking ahead, O Mighty One, but it doesn't help me out right now. Everyone in the camp is talking about it. When do I get to rule over my wife? Nobody respects a man when his wife throws clay pots at him and tosses his mat in the dirt."

God changed the subject. "You are going to name Hagar's son Ishmael. He will be born when you are eighty-six years old. Good night." God had done all of the explaining He intended to do.

"Wait," Abram cried. "Is that it? When will I hear from You again?" The rumble of thunder and flash of lightning told Abram that this conversation was over.

CHAPTER 23

THIRTEEN YEARS WOULD pass before God would speak to Abram again.

Ishmael was born and Abram loved him. Neither Sarai nor Hagar knew it, but sometimes at night, Abram would go into the desert and argue with God about how Ishmael would do perfectly well to carry on Abram's line. I wondered why Abram kept bringing the topic up as if he had to sell God on the idea of Ishmael. Sarai had been right. God did not specifically say anything about her having a child. Abram had his son; mission accomplished.

I wondered if I might be missing something in Abram's prayers, so I decided to listen more intently. Abram seemed to want God to understand how hard it was for him to be the parent of a teenager at his age.

"Can You imagine, God," Abram would say, "how difficult it would be to have another baby as old as we are?"

"Could it be that Ishmael is *not* the heir?" I asked myself. "Abram seems to have doubts."

"But he must be," I answered my own question. "Ishmael fits the only criterion God had specifically spoken about: he was from Abram's loins."

I was sure God had never said anything definite about Sarai, so I assumed when Ishmael was born, that would be it. Sarai preempted her chance by getting ahead of God. But when I listened to Abram's pleadings, I wasn't so sure. I realized that he himself didn't believe Ishmael was the son God promised. There must be another child coming.

"Ishmael is not the heir," I reported to Satan.

"What do you mean?" Satan asked. "He's Abram's son, isn't he? You said God promised him Ishmael would be the father of a great nation. So what's your point? Don't waste my time."

"God did make that promise to Abram. But apparently, that was sort of an add-on promise, a bonus son so to speak. Abram wouldn't be trying to sell God on the idea of Ishmael being his heir in fulfillment of God's commitment unless Abram knew the boy wasn't. Although he could go on to his glory in perfect contentment with Ishmael left in charge, Abram believes there is yet another son to come. Otherwise, he wouldn't be trying to talk God out of it."

Satan thought about how he could take advantage of this turn of events. He assigned two demons to dog Hagar and Ishmael everywhere they went for weeks.

"Find out where they go, what they talk about. Most importantly, do they know another child is coming?" Satan ordered.

When the two demons reported what they had learned, the information revealed nothing. They did not go anywhere. They talked and played games. They gave no indication there would be another heir besides Ishmael.

"Start with Hagar," Satan was on top of it. "You," he pointed to one of the lesser demons, "go into her tent at night. Speak into her dreams. Remind her of why Abram lay with her to start with. She would have resisted except for Abram's reassurance that her baby would be his heir. Connect the dots for her. There is another child coming, and when he comes, she and Ishmael are out."

It worked like a charm. Hagar became fearful and defensive about everything and looked for hidden meaning in what she heard from Sarai. She also treated Ishmael differently. They no longer spent their time together playing games. She went on and on to the boy about how it wasn't fair that he would never be Abram's heir. Ishmael, who didn't know what an heir was, could tell from his mother's attitude that something unjust must be about to happen. The wedge between Ishmael and the son to come was firmly established before the heir was born.

Thirteen years later, God spoke again.

Abram was now ninety-nine years old. One hot day, as he rested on a bench near his tent, the Lord appeared to him again.

"Abram," God said.

"God?" Abram blinked hard, shielding his eyes from the light now invading his shade.

Overwhelmed, Abram fell flat on his face.

Then God said to him, "This is My covenant with you: You'll be the father of many nations. Your name will no longer be Abram, but Abraham, meaning that I'm making you the father of many nations. I'll make you a father of fathers—I'll make nations from you; kings will issue from you. I'm establishing My covenant between Me and you, a covenant that includes your descendants, a covenant that goes on and on and on, a covenant that commits Me to be your God and the God of your descendants. And I'm giving you and your descendants this land where you're now camping, this whole country of Canaan, to own forever. And I'll be their God."

Wow. I had never known God to speak more than two or three sentences at one time. "Such a generous gift," I thought. "Wasteful, really. What is he going to do with such wealth at his age?"

I was impressed but not surprised at the lavish promise God made to Abraham, because it was just like Him to do something like that. He hadn't spoken to Abram—Abraham—in thirteen years, but at the end of the silence, God went way over the top to restore him into favor. Satan hated it whenever he learned God had made a covenant promise like this to a human, and I dreaded having to tell him about it. I was about to find Satan to let him know he had trouble when I realized that God was about to speak again. I dared not miss a word.

Then God said to Abraham, "This is the covenant that you are to honor; the covenant that pulls in all your descendants: Circumcise every male. It will be the sign of the covenant between us. Every male baby will be circumcised when he is eight days old."

"Whoa," I said before I caught myself.

Abraham lifted his face up toward heaven and blinked hard again. It was as if someone had awakened him from a deep sleep by throwing ice water on his head.

"Circumcised? God, are You sure?" he muttered. Abram wiped his brow and stood up, wondering whether or not this was some sort of punishment, but for what, he was not sure.

"Even the adult males, O sovereign Lord?"

God did not respond.

Maybe repentance would soften God's stand on such an extreme symbol for faithfulness, so Abraham tried again.

"I know I have made some terrible mistakes, and I've had a lot of time to think about the Hagar thing…my fault entirely. Believe me, I've paid for it already. Living with those two women is plenty of punishment. I'm really sorry I did such a stupid thing, and it is only right that You punish me. Could we not limit the circumcision to just Ishmael and me? Must we involve anyone else?"

God went on, "Every male in the house from eight days and older, free or slave, foreigner or family, all will undergo circumcision."

Abraham knelt down again. "Of course, Mighty One ever to be praised, but I should tell You that this is going to be a very hard sell. Have You seen the camel drivers lately? You can imagine how they are going to take this news."

The thunder rolled, and I knew that God was about to change the subject.

He said to Abraham, "As for Sarai, your wife, you are no longer to call her Sarai. Her name will be Sarah. I will bless her and will surely give you a son by her. I will bless her so that she will be the mother of nations. Kings will come from her."

Abraham fell on his face again, but this time it was to hide his amusement at such a notion. He laughed and said to himself, "Will a son be born to a man one hundred years old? Will Sarah bear a child at the age of ninety?"

I was about to laugh myself when I remembered it was forbidden for me to do so. Satan had disallowed it where humans were concerned. He said laughing at them could cause me to develop affection for them. As if that were possible.

But imagine how ridiculous it was. Just look at the two of them. Unless this was going to be an immaculate conception, I did not see it happening. When Abraham realized God was not kidding around, he looked up to heaven and made a request that I could understand.

"Oh, sovereign God, if only You would have favor on Ishmael. Are You sure we can't work with him? He's already thirteen. He's a good boy. Sarah would not mind; really, she wouldn't. By now she's forgotten the whole thing anyway. I don't know if I can do the diaper duty or walking the floor with a colicky baby again, not at my age." But God didn't budge.

Then God said, "Sarah is going to have a son. I'm going to establish My covenant with him."

"That's it!" I yelled out as I prepared to wing my way back to Satan's den. "I was right. There will be another son."

I waited to see if anything else was going to happen. Except for a promise to bless Ishmael as well (God rarely refused Abraham anything), that was pretty much it.

CHAPTER 24

ABRAHAM AND SARAH were about to experience what they and many after them would find to be an annoying behavioral characteristic of God. He spoke a naturally impossible promise to them and then left town for an excruciatingly long period of time when absolutely nothing happened.

Abraham and Sarah had mostly given up on the idea of seeing their promise fulfilled. Then one day, with no warning, Adonai, the second person of the Godhead, appeared in the front yard of Abraham's tent. As far as I could recall, Adonai had not set a foot on Earth since Adam.

But there He was, as real as the desert sand, standing in front of Abraham's tent with two of His warring angels at His side. I recognized Him right away, of course, but so did Abraham, which surprised me somewhat. Abraham had talked to God, but he had never actually seen Him. And who knew whether Abraham knew about Adonai? After all, the trinitarian nature of God was a theological stretch for humanity in 2000 b.c.

Abraham wasted no time in getting the whole camp into a dither to prepare a meal for his important visitors. I wanted to get close so I could hear more of what was being said, but I did not dare chance it. Those two warring angels never sat down, never took one hand off their sabers, and never stopped looking around to see who else was there, especially someone like me, a spy from the other camp. I kept my distance and strained to hear the conversation.

"Where is your wife, Sarah?" they asked Abraham. Like they didn't know.

"There, in the tent," he said.

Then Adonai said, "I will surely return to you about this time next year, and Sarah, your wife, will have a son."

Now Sarah was listening at the entrance to the tent behind Abraham. Although she covered her head with her apron and tried to muzzle herself, she laughed. But I laughed harder, despite the rule against it. I bent over into a ball, trying my best to stop laughing when I tumbled right off my perch. My balance never did improve, no matter how many times I fell off that thing. I tried to stay upright, but I'll tell you, it was hard with wings, a tail, and claws. There was not enough room to put it all.

I might have gone on giggling at the very idea of Abraham and Sarah having a baby if I hadn't accidentally rolled right over the top of Satan's tail. I hadn't heard him come up. He snatched me up by the wing and slapped the giggles right out of me, and then he demanded to know what had caused my fit.

I pulled myself together and tried to tell him what I had seen and heard. I thought he might find the whole idea as ridiculous as I had. Not a chance. In fact, he was quite stoic, showing no emotion. He lifted me off the ground and dangled me in midair while demanding to know what else had been said.

"Nothing really, master. That's it. They came to announce the baby, which we've suspected for years now, so no surprise there. There's nothing to be concerned about, I'm sure." I was gasping for air.

"Fool," he snarled at me, tightening his grip. "Adonai would not have come down for that."

"Get back down there, and find out why He is on Earth. Miss nothing. It's your head if you do."

When I returned to my listening post, the three of them were standing, and it looked as if Adonai and the angels were on their way out—or up, I suppose, is the more correct term. As they turned to leave, they looked toward Sodom but said nothing. Abraham walked along with them to see them on their way. Then Adonai stopped abruptly and turned to one of the angels and said, "Shall I hide from Abraham what I am about to do?"

"What is this?" I asked myself. When I could stand it no longer, I moved closer. They were talking in hushed and somber tones now, so I chanced it and flew in as close as I dared. I quickly ducked behind a rock when I saw one of the warrior angels tap his sword and sniff the air.

Then Adonai said, "The cries of the victims in Sodom and Gomorrah are deafening; the sin of those cities is immense. I'm going down to see for myself if what they're doing is as bad as it sounds. Then I'll know."

The men set out for Sodom, but Abraham stood in Adonai's path, blocking His way. The men continued on their way, but Adonai lingered as if intending to talk privately with Abraham, but I couldn't wait around to find out. I had to let Satan know the angels were on the way to the cities.

I was breathless by the time I reached Satan's lair. I spilled out the words as coherently as I could. "Adonai is on Earth. He's going to destroy Sodom and Gomorrah, and the destroying angels are on the way there right now."

"He cannot do it." Satan muttered. "It's against the rules. They have to be held for the day of wrath like everyone else. He cannot change the rules. He said He would not destroy the world again. Sodom and Gomorrah are part of the world. You heard Him."

He looked to the others for confirmation and all nodded in agreement, though I was certain they had no idea what he was talking about. Then Satan looked directly at me, waiting for me to nod along with the others. I looked hard at the floor as if having discovered something important there. I tried to pretend not to hear him speaking to me. My mind was racing for an answer.

"What shall I do? What shall I say?" My thoughts sped by. "I'll lie. I'll tell him he's right. No, that won't work. If I lie he will see it in my eyes. I have only one option. I'll tell him the truth and then run."

I looked back and forth, calculating the number of seconds I would need to quote the law for Satan then make it out the nearest hole before he could process what I said. Satan yelled at me again.

"You are the one who told me what He said to Noah," Satan yelled in my face. "God said that He would not destroy the world again." His eyes narrowed. "That is precisely what you told me, isn't it?"

I scrunched my head down as far as it would go between my wings and stood my scales on end to prevent him from grabbing me and swinging me around by the neck. Then I eked out the words, "Master, you are right to have interpreted it that way. Any reasonable person would have done the same. Any court would surely side with you on your interpretation."

Satan swung at me and cut me short. "Stop slobbering. Did He say it or not? Yes or no?"

I replied, "Technically, in a word, no."

Everyone went for cover. Satan's whole body was a weapon as he spewed the worst-looking stuff out of his mouth and came after me.

"You lie, you die." He lunged toward me. I stepped just beyond his grasp.

"No, no, let me explain. God said He would not destroy the *world* again by..." I could not finish before he cut me off.

"By what? Technically." He seethed.

"God said He would not destroy the world again by water." I exhaled deeply.

"Then I'm right." Satan turned and started away from me. "He will not destroy the world again. Sodom and Gomorrah are part of the world, so He cannot deal with their sin until the day of wrath—end of problem."

Satan was completely misinterpreting what God had said. His insistence that destroying the cities was tantamount to destroying the world did not make sense. Why didn't I just let him go on his way and think whatever he wanted? I never seemed to know when to stop talking.

"No, master, that is very close to right, but just the tiniest bit off, technically, of course. Not that you aren't right." I babbled, following behind him in the meekest of postures. "Of course, you always hear right. It was my fault. I did not speak it correctly."

Satan spun around and glared at me as I tried to explain what God had actually said. "The truth is, O awesome one, when God said, and I quote, 'I will not destroy the world again by water,' He left Himself some wiggle room."

"Wiggle room?" Satan asked as the other demons covered their mouths to disguise their smirking laughter.

"You know. Just in case."

"In case of what?"

"Like, just in case He was confronted with an unequivocal, over-the-top kind of sin and had to do something about it." I lowered my voice. "Sort of like what you've got going on down there in Sodom and Gomorrah. Technically, the cities do not represent His promise not to destroy the whole world. He can do whatever He decides to do locally. Wipe them off the planet if He wants, just so long as He doesn't destroy the whole world again by flood."

Satan paused for a moment as if thinking it over. He shrugged and said, "So let Him do it. Destroy them all." Satan threw up his claws as if the topic were no longer worth his time. "Why should I care whether He destroys them now or never? Their souls are mine." Instead of stalking off as he usually did, he paced back and forth, belying his professed unconcern with the matter.

"There's something more. God would not have gone down to Earth just to destroy people who are already lost to Him." Satan reasoned out loud. "If He's there, it's for some other reason. But what?" He paused as if expecting me to say something, but he went on with his monologue before I could get a word out.

"God doesn't have any people there anymore. They belong to me. And why would He tell Abraham His plans? What is Abraham supposed to do about it?"

I have to admit that I too had to think about that one for a moment. Then it hit me. "Master, think about it. Lot is in Sodom."

"And so? That means what to me?"

I continued, "Lot is Abraham's nephew."

"Lot?" Satan sneered. "Who cares about Lot? He is the great pretender, nothing close to the piety he espouses to his wife and kids. He is ankle-deep in the perversion, even if he only watches for now. It's just a matter of time until we have his pitiful little soul as well."

I was jumping around, so excited at how I had figured it all out.

"No, no. Don't you see?" I was breathless again. "Adonai told Abraham because He knows Abraham will bargain for Lot's life. How many things has God refused Abraham?"

"Do you think God doesn't know all about Lot? Why would he want Abraham to bargain for his sake?"

"Maybe God knows Abraham loves Lot?" I wondered.

"I don't believe it," Satan shot back. "That pitiful little whiner tried to steal Abraham blind. Abraham was glad to be rid of him. Abraham would not use up any points with God over that measly weasel."

I knew not to say anything else as Satan walked to the edge of eternity and stared at Earth below. Finally, he shrugged and said, "Go find out."

I flew like the wind back to Earth and dropped down behind the rock where I'd hidden before and listened.

Then Abraham approached Adonai and said, "Will You really sweep away the righteous with the wicked? What if there are fifty righteous people in the city? Will You really sweep it away and not spare the place for the sake of the fifty?"

Adonai turned away and looked back toward Sodom. Abraham hurried around in front of Him and continued.

"Far be it from You to do such a thing—to kill the righteous with the wicked, treating the righteous and the wicked alike. Far be it from You! Will not the Judge of all Earth do the right thing?"

"There are no righteous in Sodom," Adonai replied.

"But how can You know for sure? Suppose there *are* fifty righteous."

Adonai answered, "If I find fifty righteous people in the city of Sodom, I will spare the whole place for their sake."

Then Abraham spoke up again, "Now that I have been so bold as to speak to the Lord, what if the number of the righteous is less than fifty? Say there are only forty-five; would You spare the city for forty-five?"

"If I find forty-five there," He said, "I will not destroy it."

Abraham looked down as if thinking, then spoke once again. "What if only forty are found there?"

Adonai sighed and said, "For the sake of forty, I will not do it."

Abram lifted one hand as if to touch His robe, but thought better of it and didn't. Then he said, "May the Lord not be angry, but let me speak. What if only thirty can be found there?"

Adonai answered, "I will not do it if I find thirty there."

Abraham bowed down on his knees, "Now that I have been so bold as to speak to the Lord, what if only twenty can be found there?"

He said, "For the sake of twenty, I will not destroy it."

"May the Lord not be angry, but let me speak once more. What if only ten can be found there?"

"For the sake of ten, I will not destroy it, but that is it; no lower, so do not ask."

When the Lord had finished speaking with Abraham, He left, and Abraham returned home. I decided to fly toward Sodom to see what would happen.

It was midnight, and the humans should have been in their houses asleep. Most were, but not Lot. He had waited until the candles were out and his wife was asleep before rising quietly and leaving the house under cover of darkness. Lot sat by himself in the gates of the city, obviously waiting for someone. I can tell you two things about what Lot was not doing. He was not praying, and he was not expecting the arrival of destroying angels.

When the angels appeared, Lot jumped to his feet to greet them before he realized they were not whomever he was waiting for. When he saw their shimmering outline against the night sky, he became visibly nervous.

"My lords." He bowed low. "Your servant awaits your command."

"Do not bow down to us," the first angel said. Lot stood up but kept his head down, avoiding looking at the angel's face.

"We have come to destroy the cities," spoke the second angel.

"But…but why?" Lot stammered, now looking up.

"The stench of their sin and the cries of the victims of their debauchery has reached God's throne."

"I see." Lot continued to stammer. "I'm on that. I just need a little more time. I can be an influence for good here." Lot looked around nervously, suddenly remembering who was coming to meet him at the gate.

"Let's get away from here," Lot urged. "Come to my house where we can talk. Please, come right now."

Lot could not move fast enough to get the angels away from the gate lest they find out about his late-night rendezvous. The angels agreed to follow Lot to his house, but you have no idea how close Satan came to having Lot's soul sewn up that very night. Two hours later and all of history would have been different.

Lot unlatched the door and led the angels quickly into the darkened room, bumping into the table and stumbling over a bench in search for embers to light the candles. His wife awakened and came into the room to see what the noise was about.

"What is it, Lot?" she asked. "Who are these—men?"

"Nothing," Lot replied. "Nothing, go back to bed."

At that moment, loud and rude voices from outside of the house called for Lot. Someone pounded on Lot's door.

"Come out and play, Lot," said a drunken voice from the porch.

"What is that?" the lead angel asked. As if he needed someone to tell him.

"What is what?" Lot replied as he stumbled around trying to put a lock on the door.

The angel continued, "The men at the door, what do they want?"

"Them? Oh, nothing, I'm sure. Partiers on their way home who probably lost their way; they're knocking on my door by mistake." Lot fumbled with the locks.

Lot cracked the door and shouted, "You there, on with you now. We'll sort it out tomorrow."

But the men outside would not be silenced. They had seen Lot take the beautiful strangers into his house, and they salivated at the prospect.

"Bring your friends out to play with us," the voice continued.

Lot was sweating when he opened the door just enough to squeeze himself out. He motioned for them to be quiet, but his nervous state only served to incite them all the more. Soon the crowd surrounded the house.

They called to Lot, "Where are the men who came to you tonight? Bring them out to us so that we can have sex with them."

Well, there it was for the entire world to hear. The blood drained from Lot's face as he heard the angels open the door behind him and step out on the porch.

"Step aside," they said to him.

"No, masters. Wait," Lot pleaded. "It is not what you think. It isn't like that at all. I can handle this. Don't trouble yourselves. Go back inside. Sit down, eat, drink. I can do this."

The more Lot tried to hush the crowd, the louder they became. Then Lot did the unthinkable thing.

"Leave these men alone," he begged. "I have two virgin daughters who have never known a man. I will bring them out to you. Do with them as you wish, but do not involve these strangers."

Fire leapt from the angels' eyes when they heard Lot offering to sacrifice his daughters. For a moment the crowd drew back at the sight of their righteous anger.

"Get out of our way," the angels ordered Lot as they pushed him back inside his house.

"Please, let me talk to them," Lot pleaded. Once inside the house, the angels slammed the door.

The crowd grew bolder. "Look who wants to play the judge! What's the matter, Lot? Aren't we good enough for your new friends?" The crowd mocked him as they advanced. "We'll treat you worse than them."

Contrary to what sympathizers would later write, Lot could not have stopped the crowd if he had wanted to. He had no moral authority in that city whatsoever. Whatever he may have had, he lost long ago. Neither was he trying to protect the angels. He was trying to protect *himself* from the angels lest they figure out what kind of person he had become.

When the crowds grew larger and their threats escalated, Lot became truly afraid. Just then the angels raised their arms and struck the crowd of men with blindness so that they could not find the door.

In their terror at being suddenly blind, they cursed all the louder for Lot.

"Lot, what have you brought upon us?"

"Open the door. Let us in." They tried to find the way to the door but could not.

The angels took over the situation and told Lot to get his family together and leave the city. Lot had no idea how close he was to utter destruction. He stumbled around, trying to get the family to obey him, but they laughed, especially his daughters' fiancés. The boys were never fooled by their father-in-law-to-be's pretense. It was time to go, but the family would not obey.

When Lot hesitated, the angels grasped his hand and the hands of his wife and of his two daughters and led them forcefully outside through the blind and terrified men until they reached the gates of the city. I followed, determined to keep my eye on Lot.

The larger angel urged them to run. "Flee for your lives! Don't look back, and don't stop anywhere in the plain! Flee to the mountains, or you will be swept away!"

Truly frightened now, Lot grabbed his wife's hand to pull her along with him up the hill leading away from the city gates, but she drew back and broke loose from his grasp.

"I cannot go," she cried. "All I know is in the city."

Before Lot could grab her, she spun about and was turned into a pillar of salt right before his eyes.

Lot grabbed the hands of his daughters and pulled them along with him to a cave atop the hill overlooking the city. Lot and his daughters stood helplessly by and watched the cities burn.

Days after it was over, the girls tried to run away as well, but Lot would not let them go. It wasn't long after that Lot committed incest with his daughters and then blamed them.

I don't know why Abraham bothered with his nephew.

I pondered what this might mean. It occurred to me that none of this had a thing to do with Lot and everything to do with Abraham. The angels had not gone into Sodom to save a righteous family. They were there because of the righteousness of Abraham. But why? I began to put the pieces together.

"First, Adonai came down to announce to Abraham and Sarah that a baby was coming in a year," I outlined the events in my mind. "Next, He starts to leave but decides to tell Abraham how He is going to destroy the cities."

"But, why?" I said aloud. "To save Lot? If Adonai had wanted to save Lot because Lot was a righteous man, He could have done so in response to the prayers of Lot. Why involve Abraham in it?"

"Of course," I continued to myself. "Because, obviously, Lot had not prayed any righteous prayers." Lot was as guilty as the rest of them or would have been if he had stayed there another night. Given that certainty, why was Adonai so interested in saving a loser like Lot?"

"But wait," I was beginning to figure it out. "Maybe He never intended to save Lot. Adonai had been clear about what He planned to do: destroy the whole city— end of sentence. Adonai never mentioned Lot nor anyone else as a possible exception until He started bargaining with Abraham."

"What was the bargaining about anyway?" I wondered. "God knew there were no righteous people in any quantity in the city. Why play a game with Abraham?"

"Oh, my," I collapsed into a heap as I figured it out. "God was getting Abraham to pray for Lot so no one of

Abraham's bloodline would perish in the city." I knew I had the answer, and when it proved to be right, it would change the balance of power between righteousness and evil and the consequences in the human realm forever. I got myself together and trudged off to report to Satan.

Satan towered over me, demanding to know what had happened. He would tolerate no threat to his domain. I stood trembling before him, expecting to die for what he would force me to tell. He glared at me with those menacing eyes, warning me of the consequences of giving answers he did not want to hear, while at the same time demanding to know.

"Why are you holding back?" He moved closer to me. "There is more, and you know what it is. It makes no sense for God Himself to come into this realm to destroy those cities. He has no claim to anyone in there. Why did He come?"

His breath was hot on my head. "Don't tell me it was for that worthless nephew Lot. He had another reason, and you, you scoundrel, know what it is. I command you to tell me."

By now the other demons had circled us, waiting to hear my reply. "It's because God wanted Abraham to intercede for Lot to stay His hand of judgment."

"Mercy?" Satan roared.

"Something like that," I mumbled my reply.

"Impossible. Not upon the guilty." He roared again at me.

"Yes, even upon the guilty, at least for a time."

"No," he howled, "that is against the rules."

"Technically," I continued, immediately recognizing my poor word choice. "Technically, the rules He set do not limit Him in time."

"Meaning what?" he demanded.

"Meaning that He does not have to bring destruction on the guilty within a specific time period. He can wait until the day of wrath if He chooses to do so."

"But He can make no distinctions among sinners," Satan countered. "Lot is a sinner same as the rest in Sodom and Gomorrah. If He destroyed any, He is bound to destroy all for their sin. No respecter of persons and all that mumbo jumbo. By His own mouth, He said it."

I avoided the *technically* word and continued to explain the finer points of the rules of engagement that God had declared.

"His covenant states that He will do nothing on Earth except it be done in response to the request of a human being. He may do anything He wants so long as a human asks Him to do it, provided it was in His divine will to start with. When Abraham interceded for his nephew, it fulfilled the legal grounds for God to do what He wanted in the first place."

Everyone was listening, but their vacant eyes told me they had no idea the significance of what I was trying to make Satan understand.

"It was like this. Yes, Lot was in danger of judgment, as were the rest, but the intercession of Abraham, a righteous man, made it legal for God to temporarily overlook Lot's sin—a stay of execution, so to speak, in the face of judgment falling on those round about him."

"But for what reason?"

"Can only be one thing: repentance. It gives the guilty party time to repent before judgment."

It was every bit as bad as I had thought it would be. Satan was furious at the thought. He and all the rest remembered how fierce and how fast the judgment had come for us when we were thrown out of heaven because of our rebellion. Now here I was suggesting that this inferior creature, Adam's seed, could stay the hand of God in judgment by interceding for those who were about to be cast down, who, by the way, were every bit as guilty as we had been.

I almost agreed with Satan's outrage and certainly did not blame the others for their anger. I myself wanted to yell out to God, "How is that fair? Look at me. If I had been given just a moment more in heaven, I would never have followed this lunatic." But as always, I said nothing.

We didn't know how it would happen, but we knew things would change after this. How far might this prayer thing go? Certainly it had always been available to humans, but very few of them had actually used it, and until Abraham, no one could have been called an intercessor.

What would happen if this idea were to catch on? What if the righteous learned to intercede for the souls Satan had already captured? Unless he could kill them first, the intercession could buy them enough time to repent, and all of his work would be for naught.

Some of the others went into the war room with Satan to lay plans against the possibility that intercession might become more common. But I went back to my perch and stared at the abyss far below. I thought again how different things would have been for me if I'd been given a few more minutes to reclaim my sanity on the day of our rebellion. I would have made it past Michael and crawled on my belly to God's feet to beg forgiveness.

"Why was there no one in heaven to intercede for me when I needed it?" I screamed into the blackness.

No one answered.

CHAPTER 25

I T HAPPENED JUST as God said it would. Isaac was
born to Sarah. At first it looked as if they might
be one big, albeit unusual, family of Abraham,
Sarah, Hagar, Ishmael, and Isaac. But, of course, Satan
wouldn't stand for that. He sent a demon into the camp
to stir up the old rivalry between Hagar and Sarah.
Although the two women had more or less peacefully
coexisted for many years, it was easy for the demon to
agitate the bitter root between them, which had never
been removed. As long as the root remained, Satan could
rouse the ire between the women anytime he wanted.
If he thought a fight between Sarah and Hagar might
advance his plan, or if he were just bored with the whole
thing, he could whip one up in a moment.

The hurt feelings between Sarah and Hagar could flare
because each was offended by the other and neither could

do anything but feel sorry for herself. Each woman felt she had been sinned against, and each had. The problem between them could never be resolved because of the legal nature of sin. Sin against someone else requires restitution. If there is no restitution, the sin remains.

Therefore, it should have surprised no one that by the time Isaac was two or three years old, Sarah had made up her mind that Ishmael was a threat. She ordered Abraham to send Hagar and Ishmael away.

"That woman's son will not share an inheritance with my boy," Sarah declared.

"Sarah, be reasonable," Abraham tried. "There is plenty to go around. Isaac will never miss any of it."

Sarah remained unrelenting in the matter until at last Abraham agreed. He truly loved Ishmael, and the thought of sending him away crushed him. Inconsolable, Abraham went out into the desert, looking for God.

"God," Abraham cried. "Do You see what's happening here? What about Ishmael? What is to happen to him? These women will be the death of me."

God took pity on Abraham's sorrow. "Don't be so distressed about Ishmael and Hagar. Make it easy on yourself, and do whatever Sarah tells you. It is through Isaac that all I promised you will come about. Don't worry. I will make Ishmael into a nation also, because he is your son."

Hagar and Ishmael left the next day, and Satan lost interest in them for centuries.

After Hagar and Ishmael left town, Sarah settled down, Isaac grew up, and Abraham pretty much got his domestic act together. He followed God more faithfully than ever before. For the next twenty years, nothing happened of the slightest interest to Satan where Abraham was concerned. Abraham did not sin, and God protected and blessed him in everything he did.

When he finally resigned himself to the fact that Abraham was a lost cause, Satan turned his attention to Earth people who did not know the God of Abraham. They were such easy prey that he quickly tired of them and handed them over to the other demons for their sport.

It was painful to watch. Those pitiful souls were so desperate to worship something, and not knowing the true God, they were easily trapped into worshiping Satan by the antics of his hordes. The demons could get humans to do anything they wanted. The men built temples and stone images for the evil emissaries to inhabit, and Satan received the worship he lusted for. Although he protested boredom because it posed no challenge for him, everyone knew he found it intoxicating. He thrilled to see God's little dust people groveling around in front of the images they had carved, sacrificing at times their own children, begging the demons for blessing. Pathetic, isn't it?

One might think after a few centuries, it would have occurred to the people that they never got any of the things they begged and sacrificed for. As a matter of fact, their circumstances worsened; the more they worshiped the idols, the worse the demons treated them. The pitiful humans would go to any extreme to extract a favor from their stone gods. They implored and pleaded with the demonic image to punish their enemies and save their offspring, all of whom Satan had in his clutches. There was little they would not do to get in touch with the supernatural.

I expected them to resist more, but it was no time before the demons were able to convince them to offer their children as sacrifices. After that, teaching them to self-mutilate was easy. The bizarre rituals the people were willing to perform for the entertainment of Satan came from ideas the demons deposited into their wide-open minds. No life form created in God's image could have imagined doing such horrible things on its own. That was most of their problem. Earth people had lost their collective memory of being created in the image of God. Otherwise, Satan could never have forced them to do what they were now willing to do.

Satan's hordes ravished them so completely, I thought they would surely go insane or go running back in search of the God who had so lovingly created them. That's what I would have done—what I tried to do—but they never did. All of the people of Earth were in Satan's clutches. All, that is, except for the tribe of Abraham.

Given that the odds were obviously in Satan's favor—he had hundreds of tribes, and God had one—a reasonable person would have expected God to treat Abraham very carefully, even delicately, to make sure that Isaac grew up and fulfilled his destiny. If, for any reason, Abraham were to jump the fence, God would have been left with no team. No team? Game over. No question about it. If God had any chance of saving a remnant of humanity, He could not afford to call any risky plays with Abraham.

"Hold the ball, and let the clock run out." That's what I would have advised Him. I was certain this had to be His plan. Satan was so resigned this would happen that he ignored the situation entirely and allowed the demons to turn their complete attention to torturing the peasants. I alone was left to watch and wait for Abraham to die.

Years passed before God showed up again. When I heard His voice, I quite naturally assumed He was coming personally to take Abraham to eternity, but it was nothing like that at all. I had seen God require strange things of His humans over the centuries, but nothing I had seen before prepared me for what God was about to require of Abraham.

Abraham was walking in the field when he felt God's presence. Even though it had been a long time, one never forgets what it feels like when God draws near.

God said to him, "Abraham!"

"Here I am, Lord" he replied. Abraham seemed excited to hear from God again, and to be honest, so was I. Satan came right away when he heard me shouting the news. He did not want to miss the exodus of Abraham from Earth, and neither did the others. All of the demons lined up to watch. At last, Abraham would be gone, and Satan would face no resistance. He was counting down the clock when God spoke.

God said, "Take your son, Isaac, and go to the region of Moriah. Sacrifice him there as a burnt offering to Me."

A great sucking wind pulled the oxygen out of Earth's atmosphere from the cumulative gasp of both the demons who watched and from the angels who guarded Abraham. Each side was stunned by what God said.

"Sacrifice Isaac? Command Abraham to commit murder?" The murmuring traveled like an electrical current through both heavens.

"Will God defeat His own team?" a voice exclaimed.

Satan was first bewildered, then beside himself with victory lust.

"Was I right, moron?" Satan shouted at me. "Didn't I tell you there was a side to God no one else knew about? He isn't all good, now, is He? I knew He didn't really care anything about those puny humans. It was all a game. He strung Abraham along, and now that it is nearly payoff time, He turns on him."

Then Satan went off to a chant to himself as the others joined right in shouting and howling, "Satan rules. There is no god like Satan."

I walked away and sat back on my tail, trying to figure out what was happening. "Satan is *not* right about God," I said, utterly confused. "But why—what is He thinking? What does this mean?"

I don't know why I did not join in with the revelry, keep my mouth shut, and let time tell the tale. Actually, I do know why. I had been a good angel, but I was terrible at being a demon, and I could not force myself to be jubilant about any of this. There didn't seem to be any good way out of the corner God had backed into, and I felt bad about the whole thing.

I wondered if this might not be one of those faith tests God was forever demanding of people and then decided against it. If testing had been the point, God would have left an escape route for Abraham—like He always did for people—you know, in case the one being tested can't quite measure up. But there wasn't an emergency exit anywhere for Abraham.

"What will Abraham do now?" one of the demons asked Satan.

"He has only two choices," Satan bragged. "He can obey God and kill his own son, forfeit his inheritance, destroy Sarah, lose everything he's worked for, or..." Satan paused for emphasis, "...my personal favorite, disobey God and lose everything anyway because that is the penalty for disobedience when you are a chosen one." He rolled over in glee.

The demons laid bets as to which way Abraham would go. Not that they cared. No matter what he chose, Satan won. Most were betting Abraham would call it quits and disobey. We had been witnesses to the love Abraham had for Isaac and for Sarah. God's command to sacrifice Isaac was beyond all reason. The smart money was on Abraham to rebel. Satan just wanted to see someone else turn against God.

"On the other hand," Satan waxed philosophically, "there is a bonus to be had if Abraham obeys God."

"How could it get better than if Abraham were to defy God?" a cheerful demon asked.

Satan responded, "There would be no limit to the sorrow and misery we could render on Sarah and the others who would surely turn against Abraham."

"They're sure to find a way to bring him up on charges," a demon laughed.

"Or, better yet, maybe they would kill him without a trial," another chimed in.

The possibilities for devastation and chaos in the human race were endless. What Satan feared but dared not voice was the possibility that God retained a card He had not played. That's why Satan took no chances and sent his most persuasive tempter, flying at light speed to speak into Abraham's mind.

"Abraham, you've been a fool. What kind of God is this?" the demon hissed.

Abraham looked around as if expecting to see someone.

The tempter continued, "The truth is, Abraham, you have surpassed God Himself in knowledge, wisdom, and authority, and He is jealous of you."

"That is utterly absurd," I said under my breath as I watched the whole mental assault roll out. "Abraham would never believe such a thing in ten thousand years."

I could not tell whether or not Abraham was listening.

The demon continued, "Show Him what you're made of. Stand up to Him. You know what is best for your family. When was the last time He was even here? How many times have you looked for Him and He was nowhere to be found?"

Abraham looked at the ground but said nothing.

The demon continued, "Think about it. When was the last time you heard anything at all from Him? He doesn't care about you or Isaac or how this is going to make you look. You did your best; everything was on track for His promises to be fulfilled. Now, what—murder? Besides that, what kind of father entertains thoughts of killing his son? What kind of dad considers putting a knife to his son's throat as an act of obedience? How many years did you wait for a child—a son? And now you're willing to spill his blood? How can you sleep?"

I thought I saw tears in Abraham's eyes, but I could not be sure. Maybe there were tears because the demon continued to accuse Abraham to himself.

"You failed God, you know," the demon continued. "If you do this, don't expect some dramatic rescue. You made Him look bad. He never really forgave you for that tryst with Hagar. Who did you think you were fooling?"

Abraham looked to the right and then to the left, as if thinking it over.

The demon changed tactics, "You tried, didn't you? It hasn't been easy. You did your best, and all the thanks you get is the destruction of everything that has meaning to you."

Abraham stared straight ahead as the demon pressed in.

"He's made you look like a dithering old fool time after time. Remember that ridiculous circumcision business? What did that prove? People still resent you for that. What happened to that covenant? This will never stop unless you refuse to be part of His celestial insanity."

I have to say the tempter was good at his work. We could tell by the anguish on Abraham's face that he had heard every word. The betting was heating up, and the smart money banked that Abraham's faith was about to fail him; he was sure to defy God.

The others assumed I had not bet anything because I didn't have anything to gamble with—which was true, of course. The rest had territories and spoils from devastating nations and could use them as stakes in this game. I didn't have anything of value to bet with because my job was to be a watcher. One does not play for the nations if he is just a watcher. I watched and I reported; that was it. It was not necessary for me to opine which way Abraham would go, and, frankly, I was relieved no one was interested in my opinion. Anything I might have said right then would have only meant trouble for me. I knew beyond all doubt that Abraham was going to obey God, no matter who; no matter what. I don't say that I knew why he would do such a terrible thing, but I knew that he would. And, as usual when it came to humans, I was right again.

Early the next morning Abraham got up and saddled his donkey. He took two of his servants with him, and Isaac and began the long journey to the mountain God had told him about. On the third day, Abraham looked up and saw the place in the distance. Abraham and Isaac cut wood for the fire, saying nothing to each other. When they had enough, Abraham instructed his servants, "Stay here with the donkey while Isaac and I go over there. We will worship, and then we will come back to you."

Isaac, strong and tall, picked up the heavy wood and started up the mountain with his father. Tell me, where did you humans get the idea Isaac was a child and some sort of helpless victim when this happened? He was twenty-five years old. Do the math. He could have escaped at any time.

Satan was clearly taken aback by what he saw. Then a cold and fearful look of knowing came into his eyes as he looked my way. He knew what I knew: Abraham was going to obey. Satan glared at me as if this were somehow my fault. The tempter demon had failed. Abraham's faith in a God he could not see overcame his fear of the circumstances he could see.

Satan cursed and yelled at me, "Why is he like that?"

I wisely did not respond. Satan stomped his hoof, hating that he knew what would happen if Abraham obeyed God. God would rescue Abraham and Isaac. Satan turned and slapped the tempter demon for his failure and sent him tumbling through the atmosphere to Abraham's side to try once more.

"Foolish, senile old man," he seethed into Abraham's ear. "Is there no limit to your idiotic devotion to this killer God? If you do what He asks, you will kill Isaac, and your inheritance will be lost. Isaac will be dead, and

you will be blamed for it. Turn back while you still have time."

With the burden of wood, Isaac continued on ahead of Abraham, who followed with the knife in his hand.

At last, Isaac spoke up. "Father?"

"Yes, my son?"

"Where is the lamb for the burnt offering?"

Abraham answered, "God Himself will provide the lamb." He turned his eyes upward as if hoping every word he had said would be true.

Exasperated by the tempter demon's failure, Satan screamed to the spirits of fear that hovered around Earth, waiting to inhabit humans. "Go for Isaac!"

The earthbound spirits were not accustomed to hearing from Satan himself, and at first they swirled about like a whirlwind in their confusion, doing nothing more than colliding with one another. At last, they organized their attack and surrounded Isaac, looking for an entry point.

"Where is he vulnerable?" one asked another.

"Did Abraham ever abuse him?" No one could remember such a thing.

"What about lies? Abraham must have lied about something. All parents lie," said another frantically.

"Did Abraham fail him or disappoint him when he was little?" said another, grasping for anything.

They were desperate to find an emotional scar in Isaac's soul. There had to be a legal entry point before the spirits of fear could overtake him and cause him to cry for mercy.

"Better yet," one hissed. "All together, as one, let's assault him with fear. Then he is sure to turn on his father; perhaps kill him."

It could have worked out that way. Isaac was taller and heavier than Abraham. He could easily have overcome the old man.

The fear spirits continued to spin and poke, but they could not find a point of entry anywhere in Isaac.

I could have told them so, but no one would have listened to me. Satan spun on his tail in his fury at their inability to penetrate Isaac's trust in his father, but the truth was that Abraham had never given Isaac any reason to fear his father's judgment or to doubt his love. So in the face of suspicious and frightening evidence that something very bad was about to happen, Isaac continued to walk with his father up the mountain.

When they reached the place God had told him about, Abraham built an altar and arranged the wood on it. Isaac held out his arms while his father bound his son, then Isaac lay down on the stones.

"Father," Isaac began, "is there any other way?"

Abraham's eyes filled with tears as he reached out his hand and took the knife to slay his son.

Suddenly a loud voice from heaven called out to him. "Abraham! Abraham!"

"Here I am."

"Do not lay a hand on the boy," God said. "Do not do anything to him. Now I know that you fear Me, because you have not withheld from Me your only son."

Abraham looked up, and there in a thicket he saw a ram caught by its horns. He untied Isaac, and the two of them took the ram and sacrificed it as a burnt offering. God reiterated His covenant promises over Abraham and Isaac while Satan returned to his previous state of moaning, wailing, and accusing God of having broken some kind of rule.

"He told Abraham to kill Isaac," he yelled at me.

"Technically speaking," I answered, "He did not. He told Abraham to sacrifice his son, which he did. God then exercised His prerogative to provide a different sacrifice."

"You should have anticipated this," one of the frustrated demons said to Satan. Realizing his extraordinarily poor choice of words, he attempted to back up. "Not you, my lord, of course, I meant him." He pointed to me.

Needing someone to blame, they swung at me at once, but I dropped to the floor quickly, so they ended up striking one another instead. The fighting escalated into a brawl between angry demons. I was no longer important to them, so it was easy to crawl out of the den under the claw fight taking place among them. I returned to my perch and thought about what had happened.

"How long will God persist in this notion that humanity can redeem what the angels lost?" I asked myself as I paced back and forth on my branch, calculating. "How many people are on Earth now?" I wondered. "Not that it's important, because whatever the number is, Satan has more souls than God has."

Then I found myself thinking more about Abraham and this thing called faith.

"What is faith?" I mused. I failed to notice one of the other demons had tired of the fight and was standing near me.

"It is an emotion," he answered. "That is all humans know. They are governed by their feelings."

"That cannot be it," I responded, actually glad to have someone to discuss this with. "If it had been emotion, things would have gone exactly the other way. Abraham's love for Isaac would have caused him to spare his son at any cost."

"Then it is some kind of special knowledge," the demon said.

"Maybe it's like foreknowledge; the human knows in advance how things are going to turn out, so there's no risk in obeying God."

"That's probably it. Otherwise, why would Abraham have been willing to take the chance that God might really have intended for him to kill Isaac?" Then I thought some more about it.

"That can't be it either," I said, somewhat disappointed we had not figured it out.

"It's obvious God was testing something in Abraham, so if Abraham had really known in advance that nothing bad could happen, it would not have been much of a test, now, would it?"

The demon grew bored and flew away, leaving me alone to ponder the idea of faith. Whatever faith was, it had to be something Abraham clung to so strongly that he would risk his life and the life of his son.

"Faith must be more powerful than hope," I thought. "It must be more like belief."

My observations of humanity convinced me that when faced with real challenge and real consequences, you humans always act on the basis of what you believe is true, not what you hope is true. What was it Abraham believed so strongly?

"Why, of course." I finally figured it out. "Abraham believed in the character of God. Faith is as simple as believing God is who He says He is and will do what He says He will do."

"Oh, my." I exhaled slowly. "If humans ever learned they need not fear God because His character is all good and His power and His love for them are without limit and are unchanging, why, they would never fear Satan again. Earth would be lost to him forever."

I promised myself I would never think such a thought again. The very idea stirred something frightening in whatever sort of soul there might be in me. Satan was horrible. But he was all I had. If Satan lost Earth, where would I go? What would I do? God had cast me out of heaven with the rebels, and I could never return.

"God!" I screamed into the vastness of nothing. "I believe You are who You say You are. I believe You will do what You say You will do. Isn't that faith enough? Why is it enough for humans but not for me? Why don't I get a second chance?"

For the first time in my existence, I collapsed in a heap and cried.

CHAPTER 26

I CONTINUED TO OBSERVE human history for many generations. It got somewhat boring because it became absolutely predictable. After Abraham died, Satan was frantic about what Isaac might become, but the truth be told, he led a somewhat ordinary life. He married a woman named Rebekah, who had trouble conceiving, as had his mother, Sarah. Figure the odds on that, but that was the way it was. Before Abraham died, Isaac went to talk to him about the problem and to seek his advice on their childless state. Abraham was quick to tell him what was positively *not* a good course of action.

Eventually, Rebekah had twins, Esau and Jacob, who could have been poster boys for sibling rivalry. Those two never could get along, and Isaac and Rebekah did not help the matter by choosing sides. Isaac loved Esau, and Rebekah loved Jacob. Isaac and Esau were men of action while Rebekah and Jacob were schemers. In my observation of the human race, schemers win out every time.

Jacob, consistent with my theory on schemers, managed to finagle the family blessing away from Esau and married two women, Leah and Rachel. Between them, they had twelve sons and one daughter. God changed Jacob's name to Israel along the way. God was always changing names—no one knows why—but it seems important to the story to mention it.

Eventually, Israel's sons would become the leaders of twelve tribes. They would fight with the world and fight with each other. They would sin, repent, and sin again. God would punish them, and the whole cycle would start over.

Satan was unconcerned with what he saw happening since none of these boys showed any real aptitude for redeeming the fallen Earth. The most promising one was named Joseph. He made Satan nervous for a time there, but at the end of it all, the Israelites (that is what we started calling them when we weren't calling them Hebrews) found themselves in slavery to Egypt as a result of one of Joseph's ideas that seemed good in the beginning but went very bad at the end. The Hebrews were really in slavery to Satan; Egypt was just his cover story.

For four hundred years they were in bondage, and it was brutal. They were treated like animals. There were so many of them that Pharaoh was happy when some of them were killed during their labors. The truth was that he feared their great numbers, although they were no more dangerous than a flock of frightened sheep. After the first one hundred years, they stopped trying to escape altogether. The other demons had begun to complain.

"This is no fun. They don't even try to get away. There's no sport in it," the torturing prince complained. (By this time, Satan had assigned specific roles to the worst of the demons, which made it easier to know who was in charge of what.)

"I liked it better when they used to cry to God," the demon in charge of religion replied. "It was exhilarating to see their agony when they realized no one was going to answer."

In one way or another, every tribe in Egypt was in Satan's hands. The demons didn't bother chasing after the souls we already had, and the only ones we didn't have were the Hebrews. For the demons, the only fun in the whole thing was the deception and the capture. After humans were caught, the game was over as far as the rank-and-file demon was concerned. The only one who got any pleasure out of it was Satan. He received the worship he craved. None of the rest of us got anything like that.

For the demons, the world had become pretty ho-hum, except for the torture of the Hebrews, and that wasn't really any fun either—no payoff. The demons never could capture their souls. Deception loses some of its zing if there isn't a prize at the end, which with these strange humans, there was not.

The Hebrews were the only remnant of the human race God seemed to care anything about, and they had simply given up. They did not run, and they would not fight. It had been four hundred Earth years since God abandoned them, and now they were enslaved to us through the Egyptians, at least physically. I suppose I don't really know whether God abandoned them or not, but Satan insisted that He had, so all of us lesser beings, not daring to suggest that his evilness might be wrong, went right along with it. They were born slaves, and they would die slaves, and not one of them expected anything else.

Four centuries is a very long time to keep alive some vague memory of a God who is supposed to be able to rescue His people. They had no textbooks. They had no religious services. They had mud and straw to make bricks and a pitiful existence to look forward to, the same as their fathers and grandfathers and great-grandfathers had before them. They had legends of Abraham and Isaac, but did these people really exist? How could any of them know for certain?

The Israelites had become slaves and had no reason to hope for anything better. They had no cause to believe a deliverer would come to them by the hand of this same God who had allowed their disobedient ancestors to go into captivity and whose name no one could remember. They had no reason to call to a God who had done nothing on their behalf for four hundred thirty (to be exact) years. No reason to believe any of it.

Nevertheless, they did. They continued to tell one another that somehow, some way, someday, someone was coming to free them from Egypt.

In the midst of their misery, the population of the Hebrew slave nation continued to grow until at last Satan succeeded in terrifying Pharaoh with the idea of what their great numbers could accomplish if they rallied against Egypt. Pharaoh himself ordered enforced population control.

"Throw every Hebrew boy into the Nile, but let every girl live."

Satan delighted in the slaughter of children—always has. Perhaps it was because he never forgot God's promise so long ago: the seed of the woman would crush his head. Maybe that is why he tried to kill them so many times in history.

His lust for human blood was satisfied daily as he used the Egyptians to torture the Hebrews. He desperately hated that particular breed of human more than the others.

We knew why. He could not get their souls, and he could not wipe them out. In spite of possessing the souls of all of the other people on Earth, Satan was still not satisfied, and he obsessed about the Hebrews. Of course, no one would admit it, but the demons just did not get it. Hebrews were simply not worth it.

It had to be that Satan was still fixated on God's promise to Abraham about his descendants being more numerous than the sand and the stars and all that nonsense. Maybe it wasn't nonsense at the time, but it certainly looked that way now. There was no possibility these pitiful slaves could resurrect their race to fulfill the promise God had given to Abraham. That deal was dead. No one talked about it anymore.

It wasn't hard for him to cause a great lust for the blood of babies to sweep the land. People, who normally would never have considered doing such a thing, reported the births of Hebrew boys and then assisted in their destruction.

"It's for the common good," they would say to one another. "Better to die as an infant than to grow up in slavery and unwanted." They would nod and agree that if it were the law, it must be right.

I had no expectations that things were going to change for Earth. I wondered if God might be considering conceding defeat and getting on with His next project. I was thinking that very thing the morning I was at my post to watch the Nile. The Egyptians worshiped the Nile, so Satan wanted to be sure we always had some sort of disturbance going to keep their attention.

"Watch and report," the dispatching demon said to me every day. The extent of my worth to Satan could be summed up in those words. Never mind there had been nothing to report for years. I wasn't given access to the inner sanctum for any other reason than to report. I wondered if Satan would recognize me if I were to show up with any news.

The killing of the babies was certainly not news anymore. You may think the massacre would have been so awful no one could ever become used to it. You only think that way because you are human and don't understand demonic capacity for evil. Another problem is with how you're made. The painful, emotional suffering you experience when you see death, injustice, and mindless violence against those whom you consider innocent is incomprehensible to a demon. Why should anyone care what someone else suffers? Demons cannot relate to such silly sentimentality. I watched so many babies drown that I had long since lost interest and track of the numbers. It was always the same. Screaming women, screaming babies—after a while, they all ran together.

Now that I think of it, maybe that was the reason she caught my attention. The woman was not screaming, and neither was the baby she put in the basket. She was a Hebrew, no question about that. Her clothing gave her away. The baby had to be a boy, otherwise why would she be doing such an odd thing? She had probably been able to hide him for a few weeks, but now he was too big.

Although I was under orders to report the slightest variation in the Hebrews' behavior, I considered letting the whole thing slide. It didn't seem worth my effort. Why not let her try some feeble attempt to save her baby? In the end, her plan could not work because someone was sure to find the basket and turn the baby in for a bounty. Why should I get involved in a situation that was likely to resolve itself in a matter of hours? I'm certain I would have let the whole thing pass if I had not seen the baby's face.

Humans call a person's eyes the window to the soul through which one can look and see the essence of the individual. Big deal. Demons can do the same thing. In fact, they are better at it than people. They not only see, but they can also read the soul. How do you think Satan knows who the easy marks are? He sees the soul and all of its memories, scars, and weaknesses when he looks into the eyes of humans, and he always takes the path of least resistance. After all, if one is in the business of stealing souls, it helps to know what brand of deception is going to work best.

I knew something was different when I looked into this baby's eyes and could not read his soul. It was hidden from me. What I did see scared me. I had seen it only two other times in the hundreds of years and the millions of people who had passed upon Earth. I saw it in Noah, I saw it in Abraham, and now I saw it again in the eyes of this baby. No, it was not the human soul I saw in his eyes.

It was the soul of God looking back at me. I could not believe He was going to try it again, but I was convinced He was. God was launching one more attempt to save the souls of the pitiful children of Abraham.

I made mental notes as his mother placed the baby in the basket among the reeds along the bank of the Nile. His sister stood at a distance to see what would happen to him.

It wasn't long before Pharaoh's daughter went to the Nile to bathe as she did every day. Her attendants were walking along the riverbank when one saw the basket among the reeds.

"My lady," she cried. "Look, it's a basket. Shall I bring it to you?"

"Bring it," answered Pharaoh's daughter. She opened it and saw the baby. He was crying, and she felt sorry for him.

"This is one of the Hebrew babies," she said. "Where did he come from?"

As I could have guessed, the baby's sister popped out of the papyrus grass right on cue.

"Shall I go and get one of the Hebrew women to nurse the baby?" she asked, as if one might be lingering around the next bush.

"Yes, go," Pharaoh's daughter answered.

So the girl went and got the baby's mother. Pharaoh's daughter said to her, "Take this baby and nurse him for me, and I will pay you."

Now I ask you, wouldn't you think these girls might have thought this was a little too convenient? Didn't they think something strange might be going on?

Handing the baby to his mother, Pharaoh's daughter said, "His name will be Moses because I drew him out of the water."

I leaned in a bit more to take another look at the baby's face when I realized he was looking back, and he saw me. It was not possible, but across time and space, he saw me. Then he laughed. I lurched backwards, stepped on my left wing, and fell over myself trying to get away. I struggled to hurry but I couldn't get traction. I ran, I stumbled, cracked my hoof when I fell, hopped a ways on the other one, and finally got altitude.

A million questions flooded my mind. "God, where have You been for four hundred years? What makes You show up now? What are You thinking? If it's the humans You want, You've waited way too long. They are not the way You remember them. Have You seen them lately? They won't know who You are. How could the baby see me?"

I flew with all of my might to the deepest part of second heaven, where Satan reveled on his throne, but I was stopped at the entrance by his henchmen. The ranks of demons had become so defined by now that only those of high authority—the princes, powers, and thrones—could directly access Satan. I was still just a watcher. It had been a long time since anything worth reporting had occurred, so I no longer had credentials to enter in to bring news.

"I must get in," I screamed at the guarding demons.

"What do you want?"

"I know you," the other guard interjected. "You were always the troublemaker."

"I must tell him. It is important. Please, get out of my way."

I tried to rush past them, which was extraordinarily poor judgment on my part. They lashed out at me and sent me tumbling tail over claw into the wall.

"Tell him that I'm here. He will want to see me," I whimpered to them as I picked myself up. "It will be your head next if he finds that you kept this news from him."

They whispered together, and one of them went in to where the prince of darkness hid himself. In a moment the guard reemerged from the inner chambers and snarled at me.

"He doesn't want to see you. He said you are to give me your information, and I will relay the message."

In one way I was glad to let someone else give the message and let him face the wrath that would spew from Satan when he heard it. In another way, I wished

I could see the prince's contorted face for myself when he finally realized that what I had warned him about for eons was about to land on his doorstep. I thought about asking the guards to be sure Satan knew it was me who had predicted this would happen, but my good sense returned before I got the words out.

I pulled myself up and said the words that would soon enough turn his kingdom upside down.

"Tell him," I whispered, "the deliverer is coming."

CHAPTER 27

I T DIDN'T TAKE long, and it was as bad as I guessed. The gates of the inner sanctum flung open with such force that the walls on which they were hinged cracked from the weight of Satan's appearance. I had not seen him personally for quite a long time and he seemed much worse than I remembered, if you can imagine that.

"You're looking somewhat well, sir; interesting, really," I babbled, trying to figure out what was different about him. He did not acknowledge my greeting but slapped me aside and then stepped on my tail as he stomped to the edge of second heaven. I should not have said "somewhat."

At first, he did nothing. I suppose "nothing" is subject to local interpretation. In the realm of darkness, it was nothing, but to humans it might have been quite something. He stood (levitated in place is more accurate) looking back and forth with hideous eyes at who knows what, and all the while breathing sulfa and fire into the nothingness surrounding his domain. Then he began to accuse God and demand that He appear.

"Bad move, very bad move," I muttered to the guards. "What if He should actually show up here?" I could see the guards themselves were getting the jitters at the thought. I folded my wings over my eyes and hid in the corner.

"Will You never be done with them?" Satan bellowed toward the throne room of God. "What are they that You waste Your time on them? Why are they so important to You? Deal with it. They are mine, and You cannot have them back!"

I wondered if I should point out to him that, technically, the Hebrews were not his. He did not own their souls. It was the Egyptians he owned, who in turn owned the slaves. "A minor point to be sure," I was about to say, "but an important one in a court of law." Satan's snarl and low guttural growls came from somewhere deep within him.

"Maybe not." I put my head back down. He was in no mood to discuss the fine print.

In complete frustration at the silence from third heaven, Satan lurched madly into the atmosphere, chasing something that was not there. Then he crashed back onto the ledge from where he assaulted the character of God.

I stayed cowered in the corner, completely terrorized by his words. I looked at the guards who were glaring at me as if Satan's meltdown was somehow my fault. Why one of them didn't at least try to shut him up, I do not know. They knew as well as I did that Satan's ranting against the Most High God put us all at risk. There was a limit, a point, something coming one day that would mark the end of God's tolerance for this lunatic angel. None of us dared say it, but we knew it. Someday, at some time, God will have had enough. When we did not expect it, there would be a "suddenly" with God. I gasped for breath just thinking about it.

A "suddenly" of God is the thing nightmares are made of in the demonic realm. Suddenly, He would act. And when He did, it would be the certain end of this maniac and the end of us. Perhaps this was the day. I was shaking so hard that my scales began to peel off.

Satan continued, and it got worse.

"Go away, God. Go far away. Nobody remembers You here. Give them up. Find another hobby. Cut Your losses. You are not wanted. Your creation has turned against You. They worship *me*. I will kill them before I see them turn back to You. I will die before I allow them to escape."

Oh, how I wished he had not said that. "If the guards would not do something, maybe I should try," I said in my head. "We are all going to die anyway."

If socks had existed, and if I could have found one, I am sure I would have tried to stuff it in his mouth. Maybe Satan did not fear Tartaroo, the deepest part of hell reserved for the rebellious angels, but the rest of us did. I could see the demon guards were traumatized at this tirade as they shrunk back into the darkness, as if they could hide there. They were as frightened as I was at the hysteria and rage Satan was railing at the Creator of the universe.

"You think You can save them?" Satan bellowed. "Go ahead. Try to snatch them out of my hands. But it will cost You, God. Oh, it will cost You more than You are willing to pay."

Satan rolled in laughter at his threat against the Almighty, as if he had caught God in some terrible joke only they knew. His countenance changed again, and with yellow, hideous eyes, he roared then bleated as if he were some tortured animal. Next, he began frothing from his mouth and spinning on the floor like a captured tornado. He was completely mad; there was no other way to describe it.

Then as if nothing had happened at all, everything was still. I raised my head to see the guards peering out from the cave where they had sought refuge. A dreadful and dark silence cloaked us as Satan, having worn himself out from his fit, lay in a throbbing heap hanging over the edge of second heaven.

"Answer me, God," he moaned into the darkness as he settled into a motionless trance.

God, of course, said nothing.

CHAPTER 28

A s she had done for several days, Samantha waited for the phone to ring. How many weeks had it been? She read and reread the translated scrolls so many times that she could recite much of the text from memory. The hardest part was telling no one what she had. But how could she when she didn't know herself?

She had no choice but to wait. The mysterious Wonk Eman, the man without a phone number or address, would have to call her. Where was he? He had seemed so anxious to have the scrolls translated, and now he had disappeared. Nothing added up.

She answered the phone before it could ring a second time.

"Dr. Yale?" asked the voice she recognized as the strange man who had visited her so many weeks before.

"Wonk," she tried to sound calm. "Where have you been?"

"Did you translate the scrolls?"

"Yes, I did. We must talk. When can you come here?"

"I can't come. It's not safe."

"Not safe? What are you afraid of?"

He did not respond. Only the sound of his breathing assured her he had not hung up. At last he spoke.

"Someone else may try to contact you. It's desperately important that you not mention me or the scrolls."

"Who are you talking about?"

Silence.

"Wonk?" Fearing he had hung up, Samantha said, "Are you still there?"

"Yes."

"Why are you afraid?"

Wonk barely whispered, "His plan worked; he survived the flood."

Her mind raced through its stored memory of the scrolls' text to figure out who he was talking about. No one survived the flood except for Noah and his family. Suddenly she remembered.

"You don't mean Og, the Nephilim king? That's impossible."

"I'm sorry, Dr Yale. I've said too much."

"What do you expect me to do with the translation?" Her exasperation was beginning to come through her voice.

"Where are the scrolls?" he continued.

"They're safe, I assure you. I put them in my personal safe. No one has the combination besides me. You didn't answer my question."

"Yes, I know. You want to know what to do with the translation." He repeated her words back to her as if buying time to consider his response.

"Wonk, you said you knew what the scrolls contained. Is that true?"

Haltingly, "Yes."

"I don't see how that's possible. I know every person on the planet who can read cuneiform. You are not among them. Tell me what this is all about."

"It's about redemption, Dr. Yale."

"Whose? Yours or mine?"

He did not answer.

"Do you expect me to publish what I've found? Send it for peer review? What?" Suddenly exhausted, she lowered her head into one hand as she held the phone to her ear with the other.

"Not yet, Dr. Yale." His voice had a tone of concern. "Promise me you won't tell anyone yet. You don't have the whole story."

"What do you mean by that?" She was alert again.

"There are more scrolls."

"Where? How many?"

"Wait for them." He hung up.

Holding the silent phone to her ear for another moment, Samantha finally leaned back in her comfortable office chair. After several minutes, she rose and walked to her window. The sun was setting, and the Dome of the Rock shone brilliantly with the last rays of another day.